Pembroke is finally free. He spent three years in the clutches of humans who viewed him as nothing more than an animal to buy, sell, and use, but that's over now. The Rosewood pack and his brother saved him, and now, he can do whatever he wants.

If only he knew what he wanted.

Remington became friends with Pembroke's brother when Pembroke was kidnapped. Finding him has closed a cycle — and opened a new one, since Remington and Pembroke are mates.

They want each other, but they're both afraid of what Ryland will think when he finds out his best friend and his brother are together. It won't stop them from being together, but it makes everything more complicated.

As does the fact that Pamela and Fulton are still out there, plotting against the pack and the rare shifters it protects.

Strange Currents
Copyright © 2024 Catherine Lievens
ISBN: 978-1-4874-4102-9
Cover art by Angela Waters

Published by eXtasy Books Inc

Look for us online at:
www.eXtasybooks.com

# STRANGE CURRENTS
# LEGENDARY SHIFTERS 11

## BY

## CATHERINE LIEVENS

# CHAPTER ONE

"Get out there before I get angry," Colbert snapped.

Pembroke gritted his teeth and nodded. Colbert was angry because he'd caught Pembroke in his human form, which wasn't something Pembroke was allowed to do. As Colbert always said, he hadn't bought Pembroke because he was cute. He'd bought him to defend his home, and Pembroke wouldn't be of any help in his human form.

Colbert wasn't wrong. As a human, Pembroke was on the short side and couldn't fight his way out of a wet paper bag. He was thin, with no muscles to see, and it was more probable that people would laugh at him than be afraid of him.

But not in his shifted form. As a hydra, people were terrified of him. It probably had something to do with him looking like a massive dragon or having three heads. He'd been forbidden to shift into that form when he was at the auction house and hated it, but now, he was forbidden to shift into his human form. He'd gone from one hell to another and didn't even have his friend to help him through it. Pembroke had been separated from Tyler when Colbert had bought him.

He hadn't seen his best friend since then.

"What are you waiting for?" Colbert added.

He sounded angry, and life wasn't easy when he was angry, so Pembroke obeyed. He didn't have a choice. He had to get naked in front of Colbert and always did so as quickly as possible. Usually, he was already shifting before he was fully undressed. He could feel Colbert watching him, but he hadn't tried anything so far, and Pembroke hoped that would

1

continue. He wasn't sure he'd be able to fight him off him if he tried to touch him in any way.

He shook out his three heads and dropped his t-shirt to the ground. Colbert stared at him like he was an interesting insect. Pembroke didn't look back and kept his focus on the ground because the last time he'd looked straight at Colbert, the asshole had used a cattle prod against him. Pembroke's thick skin protected him from many things, but he'd still been able to feel the pain of the electricity zapping into his muscles.

He moved away from Colbert and went to place himself in his spot. It was always the same, because Colbert didn't trust him not to run if he was out of sight, even with the ankle monitor. It wouldn't be easy as a hydra, but if he got far enough, he could shift and disappear into the trees around the mansion in which Colbert lived. Colbert knew that, so he'd kept Pembroke in the courtyard at the center of the mansion. Since the estate had been built around it, Colbert could see Pembroke from pretty much anywhere in the house.

Pembroke hated it.

He hated everything about his life. He missed Tyler, but not just him. It had been years since he'd seen his brother, and he always wondered what Ryland was doing. He needed to remind himself that even though Ryland was human and they were only half brothers, Ryland cared about him. What Colbert always said about no one caring that Pembroke was gone was a lie.

Logically, Pembroke knew that, but sometimes, when he was especially homesick, he couldn't help but wonder if maybe Colbert was right. Ryland had probably noticed he was gone, but was he still looking for him after three years? Had he made peace with the fact that Pembroke would never be back, or was he still hurting over his disappearance? Pembroke wished he knew the answer to that question. It might give him more hope.

He couldn't listen to Colbert. The man wanted a slave who would do anything he asked and not rebel, and that wasn't Pembroke. He wasn't afraid of fighting back, no matter how many cattle prods Colbert had.

But Colbert could not merely hurt him but also kill him, which was what the damn plastic monitor around Pembroke's ankle was for.

It had been put on him as soon as he'd arrived here, and Colbert had told him that if he ever tried getting away from the mansion, it would electrocute him so badly that it would kill him. Pembroke didn't know if it actually would, but he hadn't been willing to test it so far. Over the three years since he'd been kidnapped from college, he'd been beaten, forced to stay in one form or another, and hurt in as many ways as the people who'd taken him could come up with. At least Colbert had never touched him in a sexual way. The memories of everything else that had been done to Pembroke made him shiver in horror, and he told himself things could be much worse than how Colbert treated him. Here, he was nothing more than a massive guard dog, and he didn't mind it as much as the other times he'd been bought.

Until Colbert changed his mind about him, anyway. If that ever happened, Pembroke wouldn't hesitate to bite his head off and try flying away. At this point, he didn't even care if he died.

Pembroke settled at the center of the courtyard. He didn't expect anything odd to happen because nothing ever did.

He was wrong.

Colbert disappeared inside, and for a little while, everything was normal. Pembroke could feel the breeze sliding over his scales, and if the situation had been different, he would have enjoyed himself. He liked being in the courtyard because it meant he wasn't inside. He could tell himself that here, he was free, even though he really wasn't.

The sound of someone running toward him made him perk up. He'd been sitting down, but now, he got to his feet and squared his shoulders, ready to face whatever was coming at him. It was probably a guard or something like that, but just in case, he wanted to be ready. His job was to protect the mansion and Colbert.

No matter how little he wanted to do it.

He was stunned when several people burst into the courtyard. He reacted instinctively since these people weren't wearing the uniform Colbert forced everyone working for him to wear. They could only be intruders, which meant it was time for Pembroke to do his job.

He stood tall in front of the group of people and stomped one foot, then another. He didn't like scaring people and making them think he was dangerous, but Colbert would hurt him if he didn't stop the intruders. They probably had a good reason to be here. Maybe they wanted to rescue one of the shifters Colbert kept as prisoners here.

Even though no one deserved to be trapped here, Pembroke couldn't allow them to do that.

He lowered his three heads to take a better look at the intruders and opened his mouths, ready to eat them even though it would take him days to feel good again if he did. He hated eating people and avoided it as much as he could. It hurt physically, but it was even worse mentally. He loathed hurting and killing people and felt guilty even when forced to do so.

One of the people in front of him stepped forward, and wings flared around them. Pembroke's eyes widened as he took in the leathery gray color of the wings that reminded him so much of Tyler. Tyler was a gargoyle shifter, and Pembroke had seen him shift many times. He wasn't the only gargoyle shifter Pembroke had ever met, and as Pembroke told himself that the odds that this was Tyler were tiny, he also couldn't help but hope.

He stared, unwilling to move until he was sure this wasn't Tyler.

But it was.

Pembroke would have recognized his friend anywhere. It had been a while since he'd last seen him, but he and Tyler had been a team against the people hurting them since they'd first met. It had been them against the world until they'd been separated.

But they weren't anymore because Tyler was standing in front of Pembroke.


Remington was at the back of the group. He didn't like it because Ryland was pushing forward, but someone had to watch their backs.

These people were nuts.

Take Tyler, for example. Even though he wasn't a fighter, he hadn't taken no for an answer when Remington had told him he shouldn't come along. Raiding this house was dangerous, and not just because of the many shifters this Colbert guy had bought over the years. There was a top-notch security system, and even though Angus had promised he could disable it, it didn't mean this wasn't dangerous.

Remington knew about danger. He and Braden, one of his two best friends, owned a security company, and they'd worked together for several years. They were used to this kind of situation, and it was far from the most danger they'd been in over the years. Most days, they acted as bodyguards, or rather, the people who worked for them did. Braden and Remington accepted security contracts and assigned their people to those contracts. It was what brought in the most money, and they all needed to pay their bills.

But it had become more than that. Three years ago, the

company evolved after Ryland asked for their help finding his brother. They still focused on security contracts, but they'd both agreed they wanted to do more. They wanted to help people who needed it and couldn't pay for it.

Like Tyler.

Ryland had been paying Remington and Braden extremely well since he'd hired them, but that was just to find his brother. Everything else like freeing Tyler from the auction house, was on the side, but Remington didn't regret it. They'd saved many people, shifters and humans alike, and he had every intention of continuing to do so.

But it wasn't easy when the people he saved decided to throw themselves at a hydra shifter. Remington was horrified as he watched Tyler push away everyone from their group and place himself in front of the hydra. They assumed it was Pembroke, but how could they be sure? There had to be more than one hydra shifter in the world, and while everything pointed to the fact that this was Pembroke, since they knew Colbert had bought him, he could have bought more than one hydra shifter. From what Angus had been able to find while digging into Colbert's phone, the man had bought and sold so many shifters over the years that it was nearly impossible to know how many he still owned.

Remington wanted to kick his ass just for that.

No one should own people, not even shifters, who had an animal side. It didn't make them any less human, and Remington wouldn't hesitate to beat up anyone who argued otherwise. He definitely wouldn't hesitate to beat up someone who bought shifters as if they were nothing more than guard dogs and servants.

"Are we even sure it's him?" someone asked from the head of the group.

Remington swallowed. They were in trouble if this wasn't Pembroke. Pembroke wouldn't hurt them once he recognized

Tyler and Ryland, but another hydra shifter wouldn't hesitate.

"Remington?" Braden's voice asked from the earbud in Remington's ear.

Remington didn't look away from the hydra as he answered. "Yeah?"

"I hope that's the guy you're looking for."

Remington snorted. "You're not the only one. How's the situation?"

"Piece of cake. Either these guards are untrained, or they're so used to nothing happening that they just don't care. We found the main security room and secured it. The hydra has something around their ankle?"

Remington squinted to take a better look. Tyler was still facing the hydra shifter, and Remington had no intention of putting himself between the two. Tyler was in his gargoyle form, which meant that he wouldn't be hurt even if the hydra attacked him. His body was made of stone at the moment.

Remington wished he could say the same, but he wasn't a gargoyle shifter. He was just a boring and ordinary lion shifter, so the hydra could kill him with one well-placed stomp of their foot.

"Yeah, I see something black around their ankle. What is it?"

"It looks like Colbert has one of those around the ankle of every shifter he bought. Not sure what it does, but I doubt it's anything good, so I asked Angus to help neutralize it."

"Probably something to keep them from escaping," Remington murmured.

"He's a dick, so I wouldn't be surprised. Since we're freeing everyone, I don't want any of these shifters to be hurt while trying to leave this place. We'll focus on this. Can you get the hydra to shift back or at least listen to you? We subdued most of the guards, but considering the number of shifters Colbert owns, I don't know how long it'll be before someone decides to attack."

"We'll be on the way out as soon as we find out if the hydra is Pembroke," Remington promised. They'd get out of here even if he had to drag every member of their group, dammit.

These people didn't seem to have any kind of self-preservation. Ryland had tried to lunge at the hydra as soon as he'd seen them without even knowing whether or not they were his brother. Tyler had done the same, but at least he was a gargoyle shifter. Ryland was a soft and squishy human, and it was a miracle he wasn't already dead after some of the things Remington had seen him do over the three years they'd known each other.

Remington's eyes widened when the hydra suddenly shifted. They wouldn't do that if they were anyone but Pembroke, right? Any other hydra would attack and try to protect themselves, which wouldn't be as easy in their human form.

Remington had seen many pictures of Pembroke over the years. Initially, Ryland had brought him a stack when he'd hired him and Braden to look for his brother. Back then, Pembroke had been nothing more than an interesting kind of shifter who needed help. However, over the three years since he'd been kidnapped, Ryland and Remington had become friends. Remington considered Braden and Ryland his best friends, and the three of them had spent a lot of time together.

Remington had heard so many stories about Pembroke and what he'd been like as a child, a teenager, and a young adult that it was almost as if he knew him. The pictures hadn't merely been pictures of a guy he didn't know after that. They'd become pictures of someone he wanted to meet, someone he felt like he already knew.

And now, Pembroke was in front of Remington in the flesh and very much naked.

He stood in front of Tyler for what felt like an eternity.

Even in his gargoyle form, Tyler wasn't very tall. Pembroke was taller, but he seemed almost frail in front of Tyler. His brown hair was too long and messy, and he was thin, almost as if Colbert didn't give him enough to eat. That would be stupid if he'd bought Pembroke as a guard dog, and Remington wondered if anyone would notice him sneaking away so he could find Colbert and beat some sense into him or beat him up, period.

He didn't like any of the people involved in this. What they were doing with the auctions and selling and buying shifters was monstrous, and Remington had already decided he'd do whatever he could to ensure these people paid for what they'd done and were still doing. He'd take down the entire operation by himself if he had to.

But he wouldn't have to. He had Braden, Ryland, and even the pack now. Rosewood had become a haven for rare shifters, and the world needed a place like that. Those shifters needed a place to call home in which they wouldn't have to fear being sold or hurt. Remington would make sure it was safe, be it the last thing he did.

Pembroke finally moved. He didn't say a word or make a noise as he threw himself into Tyler's arms. Ryland tried pushing forward like he had earlier, but someone held him back, and Remington was glad to see they all understood that, for now, Tyler was the only person safe with Pembroke.

Pembroke might have shifted back to his human form, but they didn't know what had happened to him over the past three years. They had a few details from Tyler, but they'd been separated a while ago, and anything could have happened to Pembroke during that time. He'd recognized Tyler, which was good, but there was no way to know if he would recognize Ryland or how he'd feel about seeing his brother here.

For Ryland's sake, Remington prayed that Pembroke loved

his brother as much as his brother loved him.

Pembroke didn't care that he was naked in front of a bunch of people he didn't recognize or that Colbert would hurt him if he saw him. He was supposed to be protecting Colbert's home, but instead, he was back in his human form.

The man in front of him really was Tyler, and as soon as Pembroke had made sense of that, he'd thrown himself into Tyler's arms. They wrapped around him and held him close, and Pembroke could sense that Tyler was telling him everything would be all right without using a word.

It wasn't the first time Pembroke touched Tyler's gargoyle body. It was hard, since in this form, Tyler was made of stone, but he wasn't cold. Never cold.

Tyler's scent surrounded Pembroke, and Pembroke didn't know what to do or say. It had been so long since he'd seen his best friend and felt safe that his brain didn't seem to be able to comprehend what was happening.

"You're safe now," Tyler whispered.

Pembroke didn't want to cry, but a sob escaped anyway. "I didn't think I'd ever see you again."

When they'd been separated, he'd still had hope. They'd always been sold back to the auctioneers eventually, and when they were, they could spend time together. Colbert had seen how close they were and told Pembroke to say goodbye because he'd never see his friend again. That was when Pembroke understood that Colbert would do anything to ensure he was never happy, even if he had to kill him. He'd known Colbert was telling the truth and that he'd never see Tyler again unless he escaped.

But he had. He was with Tyler now, and they were both safe.

Pembroke had known that as soon as he'd seen Tyler, but

he was even more sure of it when Tyler leaned down to haul him into his arms. They always cared for each other, so Pembroke didn't struggle or try to escape. Tyler would keep him safe.

"Get us out of here," he heard Tyler say as they started moving.

Several people were around them, but Pembroke didn't think he had the strength to look up. A part of him hoped his brother was there, but he was afraid to check in case Ryland wasn't.

He snuggled against Tyler's chest and closed his eyes. It didn't matter if Ryland was here. Tyler had come, and he'd saved Pembroke.

"You're safe now," Tyler promised.

Pembroke opened his eyes and looked at him. "I know." That was the only thing he was sure of, but whatever happened next, he and Tyler would face it together.

They moved toward the edge of the courtyard. That was when Pembroke remembered that no matter how hard Tyler would try to keep him safe, he might fail because of Colbert.

"There's something around my ankle," he said as he tried pushing away from Tyler. He didn't want Tyler to be hurt if he was going to explode or be electrocuted.

"We already took care of that," someone said.

"What is it?" Tyler asked.

"We're not sure, but it was clear Colbert used it to keep these people here, so we neutralized every single one of these things."

"He said it would kill us," Pembroke explained.

Tyler's expression turned hard. "Not on my watch. I'm going to kill *him*."

"You'll do no such thing," a voice Pembroke recognized said. "Your focus needs to be on Pembroke right now. We'll take care of Colbert and every one of his guards and the people he works with."

Pembroke was almost afraid to look, but he did. He couldn't *not* check if his brother was here now that he'd recognized his voice.

He turned his head. He was both surprised and not surprised at the sight of his brother walking next to Tyler. He wasn't focused on him, but maybe he felt Pembroke staring, and he turned to look.

Pembroke gasped. He remembered his brother as a young man full of dreams and hope, even though he was older than Pembroke by fifteen years. At thirty-seven, he'd appeared younger, but after three years, Pembroke could see every single one of Ryland's forty years etched on his face.

Had he been the one to do that? Did Ryland look like this because of Pembroke's disappearance?

"It's good to have you back," Ryland said.

Pembroke couldn't answer. He opened his mouth, but he didn't know what to say. He wanted to tell his brother that he'd missed him and that he'd hoped for the past three years that Ryland would find him, but the words wouldn't come. Thankfully, Ryland seemed to understand. He patted Pembroke's naked knee, then turned his focus back on where they were going.

"We'll have time to talk soon," he promised.

They would, because Pembroke was free. He was free because his brother and his best friend had come for him, and they'd done so because they loved him. Every single word Colbert had said about them had been a lie.

He wanted to find Colbert with Tyler and ensure the man never hurt anyone else.

Now that he knew he was safe, Pembroke peeked around Tyler. He'd known they weren't alone because he'd heard several voices, but he could see the group was more numerous than he'd expected. Tyler and Ryland were part of it, along with three men Pembroke didn't recognize. He didn't think he'd known them before being taken, but they seemed familiar with both Ryland and Tyler, and the way they moved told Pembroke that they knew what they were doing. They were clearly professionals, which made sense. Neither Ryland nor Tyler could have done this on their own. They wouldn't have known where to start unless something had changed while Pembroke had been away.

He tried to imagine what had happened. When he and Tyler had been separated, they'd both been locked up in cages at the auction house. Somehow, Tyler was free now and had ended up with Pembroke's brother.

*How?* Pembroke wanted to ask, but he could hear screams in the distance, so he snuggled harder against Tyler.

He would keep Pembroke safe.

"What's going on?" Ryland asked.

"Braden and the others are working," one of the men Pembroke didn't know said.

He pressed a finger against his ear, and Pembroke realized he was listening to something. The guards around the mansion also wore earbuds, so he'd seen this before.

"They're freeing as many shifters as they can," the man continued. "Apparently, some of them decided to get revenge on the guards."

Pembroke grimaced. He'd been working with these shifters since he'd arrived, and he knew how angry some of them were. If they were free to roam the mansion, it would be a miracle if the guards and Colbert made it out alive.

He didn't care.

Pembroke stared at the man with the earbud. He was walking close to Ryland, and it was clear from the way they moved that they were comfortable around each other. They didn't react, even when they brushed against each other as they walked.

The man was as tall as Ryland, who was six foot two. His shoulders were wider, and even though they both wore black clothing, it was clear this guy was much more muscled than Pembroke's brother. He seemed to be around the same age as Ryland, and his dark hair was cut short. The thing that Pembroke liked the most was his startlingly light-blue eyes. Every time he glanced at Pembroke, it was as if he could see right through him and find his deepest secrets.

Pembroke hoped that wasn't so.

"I don't want anyone to come out of this alive," Ryland declared.

His voice was harsher than Pembroke had ever heard it. His disappearance had hurt Ryland, and Pembroke couldn't find it in himself to tell him not to give that order.

"I'm pretty sure the shifters Braden freed will take care of that for you," Ryland's friend said.

"I don't know if it's enough. It doesn't feel like it is."

"They'll take care of the guards, but you have to find Colbert," Pembroke said. "He's the dangerous one. He has a lot of money and many houses, so he can sneak away and start buying shifters again if you don't stop him."

Ryland's friend grinned. "Even if he survives this, he won't be able to do much, since we have control of his bank accounts."

Pembroke stared in shock. How had Ryland and Tyler ended up with these people? What the fuck was happening?


Remington had to work hard not to stare at Pembroke, especially when he realized that Pembroke was watching him. For some reason, Ryland's brother seemed fascinated by Remington, and while Remington didn't understand, the thought was enough to make him want to puff out his chest. His lion was pleased. Remington gave it a quick smackdown so that the beast would know to stay where it was. The last thing Remington needed was a spontaneous shift because his damn lion wanted to preen in front of Pembroke.

It was odd, because his lion had never reacted like this to anyone. Remington had been in control of his shift since he was a teenager, and he wasn't planning for that to change anytime soon. He needed to be on guard, especially in this situation.

Since he was distracted by Pembroke, he moved forward in the group. Bryson was at the back, with Ryland, Tyler, and Pembroke in the middle and Mercer and Remington leading. Remington was listening to Braden, while Mercer had an earbud that connected him to Angus, the Rosewood hacker. He'd been the one who cloned Colbert's phone, to find out about this mansion and its security system, and to hack his bank accounts. He'd make sure Colbert couldn't even buy himself breakfast, let alone a rare shifter to guard him.

That thought was more satisfying than thinking about killing him. Death would be painful, but it would also mean Colbert didn't suffer nearly enough. After what he'd done to these people, Remington wanted him to feel what they'd felt. Taking away his money wasn't enough, but it was a start.

Even though Remington trusted Braden with his life, he held his breath as they crossed the gates that circled the mansion. It was open now, so they didn't have to climb the wall. Braden had said that the ankle monitor on Pembroke was inactive, but there was still a hint of fear and worry in Remington as they walked through the gate.

Nothing happened.

Remington breathed easier. Like always, Braden had come through. Remington couldn't worry about his friend right now. His priority was the three men walking behind him and getting them back to Rosewood and the pack's safety.

When they'd planned this, everyone agreed that they'd

each have their own role and job. Remington and the Rosewood pack members would focus on getting Pembroke back. He was the reason they were doing this, and Ryland would have bitten off the head of anyone who would have suggested otherwise.

They'd all agreed they couldn't abandon the other shifters Colbert had bought, though, and that was where Braden had come in. He had enough men to go through the mansion, find every single one of those shifters, and free them. That was why Remington didn't hesitate to leave him behind. He and their men would find their own way out. Their vehicles were parked around the mansion, and they knew what they were doing. Remington wasn't worried about them.

He was only worried about getting Pembroke back to Rosewood.

They finally reached the van in which he and the Rosewood pack members had arrived. Mercer rushed forward to unlock the doors and check the van while Tyler made a beeline for the back of it. Remington got there first and slid open the door, and he watched as Tyler gently deposited Pembroke in.

"We brought you some clothes," Ryland said as he climbed into the van to grab the backpack he'd left there. "I wouldn't have thought about it, but Tyler did."

"Tyler always thinks of everything," Pembroke murmured.

His voice was soft, almost like he was afraid to speak up. Was it because of something Colbert had done or said?

Once again, Remington resisted the urge to run back into the mansion and find the asshole. If he was still there, Braden would find him. Remington wasn't sure what they would decide to do with him if they did, but he wouldn't be the one making the decision.

Remington, Mercer, and Bryson kept watch as Pembroke

dressed. Tyler had shifted back, and he and Ryland were fussing over the hydra shifter. If Remington hadn't seen it with his own eyes, he wouldn't be able to believe that such a sweet, gentle-looking man could turn into a hydra with three heads and more fangs than Remington had been able to count. He'd seemed dangerous then, but now, Remington's instincts screamed at him to protect the man.

That wouldn't go down well with Ryland. Remington didn't know how the relationship between the brothers had been before Pembroke was kidnapped, but he could already tell that Ryland would be overprotective now that he had Pembroke back. Remington didn't blame him, but he hoped Ryland realized that Pembroke might not be okay with that and that he wouldn't try to smother him with love and protection.

Pembroke had been taken away three years ago, and he'd had to be strong to have survived for so long. He was probably all right with his friend and his brother fussing now, but something told Remington that wouldn't last long.

More shouting made him jump. From what Remington could hear through the earbud, Braden and their people were all right, but he didn't like the sound of what was happening. He needed to take Pembroke, Tyler, and Ryland away before the fight reached them. He didn't want to rush Pembroke, but they could reunite in the van or back in Rosewood territory.

"We have to go," he told Ryland.

Now that his brother was back, Ryland looked almost younger. There were still dark shadows under his eyes, and he was frazzled, but the smile on his lips made him look like a different man. Remington had seen Ryland smile and had heard him laugh over the past three years, but never like this, as if he was truly happy.

"I'll stay in the back with Pembroke," he said.

Remington wasn't surprised. "I'll drive. You get in the back with Pembroke, Tyler, and either Mercer or Bryson. The other will ride with me in the front."

"I'll sit in the front," Mercer said as he climbed into the passenger seat.

Bryson shrugged as if he didn't care and got into the back of the van. Pembroke was dressed now, but he was moving slowly as if he couldn't quite trust what was happening. He probably didn't, even though Tyler and Ryland were there. After everything that had happened to him, it had to be hard to trust anyone, even people he knew.

"We're going to Rosewood," Remington explained quickly as he climbed into the driver's seat and turned to Pembroke. "There's a pack there. Mercer and Bryson are part of it, and their alpha has been helping us to find you."

Pembroke stared for a moment before nodding. "Thank you for telling me."

"It's fine. I figured you'd want to know where we were going. Now settle in. There's food and drinks if you want, and I'm pretty sure your brother packed a pillow and blankets."

Pembroke grinned. For the first time since Remington had initially seen him, he didn't look in shock. He looked happy, and the sight made Remington smile back.

"Come on," Ryland interrupted.

Remington almost rolled his eyes, but it didn't matter. They needed to start moving.

They all got situated, and Remington finally managed to drive them out of there. He didn't relax until they were far enough away from the mansion that he was sure Colbert wasn't coming after them. He wouldn't have put it past the asshole.

Mercer relaxed in the passenger seat, too. He even smiled, something Remington didn't think he'd ever seen.

"We did it," he said.

Mercer nodded. "We did."

Remington glanced in the rearview mirror. Pembroke was sitting on one of the benches in the back of the van, bracketed by Tyler and Ryland. Someone had wrapped a blanket around him, and he was gripping a water bottle. Ryland had an arm wrapped around his brother's shoulders, while Tyler had hooked one of his around Pembroke's waist. It was as if they didn't want to let him go, and Remington understood them perfectly.

He'd seen how badly Ryland had taken his brother's kidnapping and how much he'd tortured himself over the years. The only thing he'd ever wanted was to get Pembroke back. The fact that he had and that Pembroke seemed to be okay was a minor miracle.

But it had happened, and Remington almost couldn't believe it.

# CHAPTER TWO

Pembroke had no idea how long they stayed in the van. He was probably in shock, but he wasn't sure what to do about it or even if there was anything he *could* do. He felt like he couldn't move, and the only thing he could do was allow Tyler and Ryland to coddle him.

He felt he'd earned it after being away from his brother for three years. He didn't know how long it had been since he'd last seen Tyler, but it had been too long, and he hoped he never had to stay away again. He had no idea where they were going, but he trusted Ryland and Tyler, so it didn't matter. Wherever they were headed, they'd make sure Pembroke was safe and protected.

That was all that mattered to Pembroke right now. It had been too long since he'd felt safe, and he suspected that was why he felt sleepy. Back with Colbert, he'd slept when allowed but never deeply, and he'd had nightmares. He'd been terrified about what would happen if anyone walked into his room while he was unconscious, and he was pretty sure that the fear had worsened the nightmares.

It would be impossible for someone who had been through what he'd been through not to have nightmares. He had it better than a lot of other shifters who were bought and sold, but that didn't mean his three years had been a walk in the park. He had the scars to prove that it hadn't been.

So he gave himself the length of the car ride to get himself together and get some rest. He didn't know what awaited him once they arrived, but he wasn't afraid, just anxious. He'd need to learn to live again. His past life had been ruined by the people who'd kidnapped him, and he didn't have anything of it anymore. The only thing he could do was look to the future, but even that made him nervous.

What if he didn't have a future? What if he never managed to recover from what happened to him? The thought was terrifying, and he found himself feeling like he couldn't breathe.

"Relax," Tyler murmured.

"I don't know if I can."

Ryland's arm around Pembroke's shoulders tightened. "Just tell me what you need, and I'll make sure you have it."

It was a promise, and even though Pembroke hadn't thought it would help, it did. "I don't know what I need," he whispered. His eyes burned. He was going to break down and let it all out because it was a long time coming, and there would be no better people to do so with than Tyler and Ryland.

"How did the two of you end up together?" Pembroke asked, hoping they'd distract him.

"We'll tell you everything once we arrive," Ryland promised. "I know this is scary, but I swear you're safe. No one will ever be allowed to touch you ever again."

Pembroke wanted answers, but his brother's promises had the effect he'd hoped for. He felt his body relax, and he leaned his head against Ryland's chest. Ryland held him close, along with Tyler, and Pembroke was surrounded by people he cared about and who loved him.

He fell asleep.

Pembroke woke up when he felt the van stop moving. He'd been asleep, but not deeply, so he'd heard the people in the van with him speaking softly. He hadn't been spying or paying attention, but it felt safe, which wasn't something he was used to anymore. He didn't want to leave the van. It was the first place where he felt safe since being kidnapped three years ago, and he was terrified of what he'd find outside.

"Where are we?" he asked.

Ryland smiled down at him. "We reached Rosewood. The pack and its alpha are friends of ours, so you'll be safe here. Remington and I have been staying with the pack, but now that I have you back, we can go home."

"Or you could stay here with me," Tyler said as he glared at Ryland.

Pembroke rolled his eyes. "Don't start fighting. I don't know what I want to do except eat something and sleep for twelve hours."

"Of course," Ryland said quickly. "I'm sorry. It's just that I've been looking for you for three years, and I'm not sure how to behave now that I have you back. The main thing I want to do is protect you, and I feel that would be easier to do if we were home, but I understand it might not be what you want."

Pembroke sighed. "I don't know what I want." And something told him it would be a while before he found out.

The other men in the van were already moving. The one who'd sat in the back with Pembroke, Ryland, and Tyler got to his feet and slid open the door. Pembroke blinked at the sudden light but quickly focused on what he could see outside.

They were parked in front of a house. It wasn't huge, but it looked comfortable, and nestled as it was between the trees, it was beautiful. Pembroke didn't know much about packs, but he did know that most of them lived in nature, and this one didn't seem to be an exception.

The man who'd opened the door hopped out of the van, leaving Pembroke with Tyler and Ryland. Tyler was the next one to go. He got out but didn't step away like the other guy. Instead, he held his hand out, and Pembroke knew he expected him to take it.

He did.

He pushed away from the bench and Ryland, tightened the blanket around his shoulders, and took Tyler's hand. Tyler helped him out of the van, and as soon as his feet were on the ground, Pembroke huddled close to his best friend. He looked around, not surprised by what he could see.

The house in front of which they'd parked wasn't the only one there. There were others on both sides of it, and from what Pembroke could see, they'd been built in a semicircle with a big fire pit in the middle. He could see more houses hidden among the trees, and the place made him want to explore.

"You're going to meet a lot of people you don't know," Tyler murmured as he rubbed his hand up and down Pembroke's arm. "No one will be offended if you don't remember their name."

For now, Pembroke hadn't learned even one of them. He looked back at the van, and his gaze caught with the gaze of the man who seemed to be Ryland's friend. "I *want* to remember them," he told Tyler. "Especially the names of the people who were there when you saved me. Who are they?"

Tyler nodded. "The man who was in the back of the van with us is Bryson. He's a wolf shifter. The two guys in front are Remington and Mercer. Remington is a lion shifter and your brother's best friend. Mercer is part of the pack, but I don't know what kind of shifter he is. Now that I think about it, I don't believe I've ever seen him shift. I assume he's a wolf, but I might be wrong, considering how many rare shifters are part of this pack."

Pembroke nodded. From what Tyler was saying, the pack seemed like a nice place to live. If anything, it welcomed rare shifters who didn't have a place elsewhere and risked being kidnapped by people like Colbert.

Pembroke should know since that was what happened to

him.

He now had the name of the man who'd fascinated him since he'd first seen him during his rescue. He'd been right when he'd thought that Remington was Ryland's friend.

"And these are Cam and Toby," Tyler continued as he gently turned Pembroke toward the house. "Cam is the alpha of this pack and a wolf shifter. Toby is his mate and a unicorn shifter."

Pembroke blinked. He'd met several unicorn shifters over the past three years. They were rare and had the power of healing, which was why people wanted them.

"Hello, Pembroke," Toby said in a gentle voice. "It's good to meet you. Are you hurt anywhere? Can I heal you?"

Pembroke shook his head. "I'm fine."

Ryland made a small sound from where he stood behind Pembroke. Pembroke knew him well enough that he understood it meant that his brother disagreed with what he'd said. Pembroke had been naked when he'd shifted earlier, so his brother would have seen the scars. Pembroke didn't think he was up to explaining them yet, but he could reassure his brother.

"I'm not hurt," he promised. "I have scars, but they're old wounds, so there's nothing even a unicorn shifter can do about them." He smiled at Toby. "But thank you for asking."

"Hello, Pembroke," Cam said as he stepped closer.

Pembroke noticed he kept a respectful distance, almost as if he was afraid that Pembroke would freak out if he came too close. He was a big man and intimidating, but he was a shifter. The people who'd hurt Pembroke had almost always been humans, although he'd met his fair share of awful shifters. These people didn't seem like they were part of that group. Cam had taken a unicorn shifter as his alpha mate, and Toby seemed healthy and happy.

Maybe Rosewood *was* a haven for rare shifters. Pembroke

had doubted it even after it had been mentioned earlier, but now that he was here, he had hope.

He wasn't an idiot. He knew that if he went back to his old life, the risk of being taken again would be high. He'd been living alone, without the protection of a pack or even his family. Not that there would have been a lot of protection coming from them. The only one who cared was Ryland, but he was fifteen years older and had his own life. Pembroke wouldn't ask him to drop everything just to keep him safe, meaning he needed to find a safe place. Maybe this pack would be that place, or maybe not.

Only time would tell.

Remington's job was done. He'd taken Ryland and the others to Colbert's home, and they'd saved Pembroke. That was what he and Braden had been paid to do three years ago, and he was satisfied, but at the same time, he felt he wasn't done yet.

He wasn't just a guy Ryland had hired anymore. He was his friend, and he told himself that was why he wasn't ready to leave. He wanted to check in on Ryland and make sure both he and Pembroke were all right.

Even if they weren't now, they would be. The Rosewood pack was safe, so they'd have protection, and Pembroke would have everything he needed to recuperate both physically and mentally. It wouldn't be easy after what he'd gone through, but he was a strong man.

He was also beautiful.

Remington looked away from Pembroke. Even though Pembroke was an adult, he felt like an asshole thinking of him that way. He'd been kidnapped and hurt, and the last thing he needed was for Remington to drool after him.

"He caught your eye," Mercer said as he leaned against the

van.

He was watching his alpha and the alpha mate welcome Pembroke. Remington still wasn't sure what to think of Mercer. Even using his nose, he couldn't tell what kind of shifter Mercer was. He wasn't a wolf, but that was all Remington could say. He'd decided that Mercer was probably a rare shifter who didn't want everyone and their mother to know what he was, and that was all right.

"I don't know what you're talking about."

Mercer snorted. "Sure you don't."

He was observant, and Remington didn't like it. "He's too young for me, and he's my best friend's brother. More importantly, he's just been through three years of hell. It doesn't matter that he caught my eye and that I find him adorable."

Mercer was silent for a moment before nodding. "I get that, but it doesn't mean you need to stay away."

"I believe it does."

"I usually stay out of people's private lives, but I can see that all of you are going to want to coddle Pembroke. It might be what he needs, but it also might not be, so I don't want you to be surprised when he explodes."

Remington frowned. "What are you talking about?"

"Exactly what I said. I understand what he's going through and that he's young, but being young doesn't mean he doesn't know what he wants or that he can't fend for himself. He's going to want to be treated like an adult who knows how to survive because that's who he is. He might be Ryland's baby brother, but he's in his mid-twenties and survived things stronger men than him didn't. Don't let his youth fool you. That man is strong as hell."

Remington agreed.

"Why don't we all go inside and sit down with something to drink?" Toby asked.

"I'm out of here," Mercer declared. He waved at his alpha.

"You know where to find me if you need me. Can you let me know when the others come back? I'm curious to find out what happened after we left."

Cam nodded. "Of course."

Bryson had already left, so that left only Remington. He cleared his throat to get Ryland's attention. Ryland was more relaxed than Remington had ever seen him. "I'll head out, too. Maybe Braden needs my help."

Ryland frowned. "Why would you leave? Don't you want to sit with us?"

"I thought it would be better if this was a family reunion." And Remington wasn't part of the family.

"You're my best friend, just like Tyler is Pembroke's best friend. That makes you family."

Remington was touched but still hesitant. He looked at Pembroke, whom Tyler was gently guiding toward the house as they followed Toby and Cam inside.

This was going to become a problem if Remington wasn't careful.

He didn't want to hurt Ryland by seducing his baby brother behind his back, but he wanted to hurt Pembroke even less. He saw him as a young and fragile man, but as Mercer had pointed out, he was anything but. He was an adult who'd gone through hell, and while he'd need support, he could make his own decisions, especially when it came to relationships. His free will had been taken from him for too long.

But Remington's thoughts were rushing ahead without a reason. Pembroke had caught his eye, but he doubted Ryland's brother had noticed him. To him, he was probably just the guy who'd been driving the van.

And that was perfectly fine.

"As long as you're sure," he told Ryland.

Ryland wrapped an arm around Remington's shoulders

and pulled him toward the house. "I wouldn't have asked if I wasn't. Pembroke wouldn't be with us today if it weren't for you and Braden. You especially put a lot of work and time into finding him, and I can never thank you enough for that."

"It was my job, and you paid me handsomely to do it."

Ryland gave Remington a little shake before letting go. "Don't be an idiot. I know that this became more important than just a job over the years."

"Because you're my friend." Remington would have done everything he could without Ryland paying him and Braden, but Ryland had always insisted they needed to be paid for their work.

They had been, and now, that work was over. Pembroke was back with Ryland and ready to start a new life.

Since Toby had mentioned getting something to drink, they headed to the kitchen once they were inside. Pembroke and Tyler were already sitting at the table while Toby was moving around the room and handing things to Cam, who put them on the table. Pembroke was leaning against Tyler's side, and Tyler was hugging him with one arm while gently talking to him.

It was good to see that Pembroke had so many people who cared about him. It would have been impossible to rescue him otherwise.

That made Remington think of the many shifters who didn't have anyone looking for them. They were kidnapped, sold, and bought, and no one ever looked for them. The thought was enough to make him want to kill someone, preferably Colbert and the people involved in the auctions.

No one deserved to go through that, and no one deserved to be bought, sold, and used in the worst way a human being could use another. It didn't matter if Ryland decided to stop paying him now that Pembroke was back. Remington would continue working to destroy the auction house and free all the shifters that had ever been through it.

"I didn't expect a pack to be involved," Pembroke said.

Since everyone was getting settled in their seats around the table, Remington rushed to do the same. He ended up in the seat in front of Pembroke and couldn't look away.

Pembroke had pushed away from Tyler, but both Tyler and Ryland hovered close as if they expected him to need them. Pembroke's fingers were wrapped around a steaming mug that smelled like hot chocolate rather than coffee. It was probably a good idea not to give Pembroke caffeine.

"Because I'm human?" Ryland teased as he gently knocked their shoulders together. "I know, it's a surprise."

"How did it happen?"

"Well, when you were taken, I didn't know where to start looking. I tried on my own for a little while, but the police weren't interested. They said you were an adult and had probably decided to drop out of college or something. They told me to return if you didn't come back, but I decided that even if I did, they wouldn't be serious about finding you. Besides, I suspected your disappearance had something to do with the fact that you're a hydra shifter, and I didn't want to tell them that. I needed someone else, which is how I found Remington and Braden."

Pembroke turned his attention to Remington.

The way he looked at him took Remington's breath away, and he found himself raising a hand and wiggling his fingers in hello. He almost swore out loud at how stupid that was.

What was it about Pembroke that flustered him so much? It couldn't be because he was gorgeous and strong, could it?

What the fuck was happening to him?

Pembroke had been curious to know how his very human brother had become friends with a lion shifter. Now he knew and was so grateful that he could have kissed Remington.

He wouldn't have kissed him just because of that. Remington was handsome, and it had been a while since Pembroke had allowed himself to notice any man. It had been too dangerous while he was at the auction house or with Colbert, but now, he couldn't look away.

"I hired them to find you," Ryland continued, clearly not having noticed Pembroke's interest in his friend. "I think that it became a question of honor for them after a while. It wasn't easy, and while we were searching, we found the pack. They had a reputation for helping rare shifters, and I thought that if there was anyone who could help us find you, it was them."

Pembroke forced himself to turn his attention back to his brother. "How did you end up with Tyler? The last time I saw him, he was in a cage at the auction house."

"Your brother bought me," Tyler said.

Since Pembroke knew Ryland would never hurt anyone, he didn't start yelling at his brother for buying someone. Besides, Tyler's voice had a teasing tone that told Pembroke he was fine with how things had gone.

"We heard about the auctions and decided to go and see if we could find you," Ryland explained. "That's where I saw Tyler. He was put on auction, and I couldn't leave him there. I wanted to buy every single shifter, but I couldn't. I don't know what made me buy him of all people, but I'm glad I did because he told us about you. He knew who'd bought you, and from there, it was fairly easy to find you."

Pembroke didn't allow himself to think of what would have happened if his brother hadn't bought Tyler. He'd probably still be with Colbert, guarding his home.

Part of him had a hard time believing he was really free. He expected to wake up and realize it had all been a dream. That happened sometimes, although the nightmares happened more often. In a way, Pembroke felt that even the dreams in which he'd been reunited with Ryland had been nightmares. Every time he woke up from one of them, he felt like his life was burning down around him all over again.

"We agreed to help Ryland because it was the right thing to do," Cam, the alpha, explained. "Our pack has become a safe place for rare shifters over the years. It started with one, but now, we have a lot of them, and I want this pack to be a place they can call home and build a life without worrying about what will happen to them. I want all of them to know that if someone ever gets them, we'll get them back." He wrapped an arm around Toby's shoulders and pulled him close to kiss the top of his head. "What these people are doing isn't right, and we'll fight to free every single shifter they've captured and sold."

It was overwhelming. When Pembroke had allowed himself to think about what would happen if he was ever freed, he'd always focused on himself. It had been bad enough without having to focus on the others, too, although it made him selfish. Now that he was free, he wanted everyone else to be, too, but he didn't know if he'd have the strength to help. He wanted to, but he was also terrified that putting himself in that situation would send his mind right back to the three years in which he'd been a prisoner, and he didn't want to break down.

He was finally free. If he had a choice, he would never go back.

"Can you tell us what happened to you?" Ryland asked gently.

Pembroke closed his eyes. There was nothing he wanted less than to tell his brother and the other people around the table what had happened to him. He didn't want to relive that pain, but he understood it might be essential to save the others.

Tyler wasn't the only friend Pembroke had made over the

three years since he'd been taken. He'd met many shifters, both rare and not, and they'd all been in the same position. He'd grown close to some of them and wanted them to be free, whatever it took. Although he wanted to try, he might never be able to do anything physically, but maybe telling his story would help anyway.

He opened his eyes but couldn't look at anyone, so instead, he kept his focus on the hot chocolate in his hands.

"You already know the beginning of it. I don't know how these people found out I was a hydra shifter. I was careful never to tell anyone in college because I didn't want to be different. I shifted as little as possible, but I guess someone could have seen me and blabbed. I wasn't aware that anyone knew what I was, so I wasn't careful. They got me one evening while I was going back to my dorm."

It was as if Tyler and Ryland couldn't stop touching Pembroke, and Pembroke was glad for that. He needed their strength to get through this.

"They stuffed me into a van and covered my head," he continued. "They didn't tell me who they were and what they were doing, no matter how many times I asked. I was in a cage when they finally got me out of the van and took the cover away from my face. There was this guy, Fulton. He was walking around the cage and looking at me as if he was appraising me."

Pembroke had felt like an animal, and not just because of the cage. It had been clear in the way Fulton treated him and even looked at him that he considered him nothing more than an animal to be sold for profit.

"I've met him," Ryland said. "He's a dick."

Pembroke grinned. "I've called him much worse. He quickly sold me, and I left the auction house." Pembroke sucked in a breath. "I was used in illegal fights."

Someone around the table swore, but Pembroke didn't

look up to see who it was. This was the worst bit of what had happened to him, and he wanted to get through it.

"There are illegal fights in which people use shifters instead of animals. I saw many different shifters while I was there, most of them normal shifters like bears and lions. Their owners had them fight against each other, sometimes to death."

Pembroke squeezed his eyes shut again. He'd been ordered to kill many times, and he'd known that the only other alternative was to be killed, so he'd done it. He didn't think he'd ever be able to forgive himself, but maybe he wasn't supposed to. Maybe he should carry the guilt until he could avenge the people he'd been forced to kill.

"That's where I got the scars," he explained. "Usually, I had to fight against big shifters like bears and lions, sometimes dragons. I was so big that often the owners had to pair two or three shifters to fight me. I was lucky because I survived all my fights, but not everyone does."

"How did you end up back in the cage at the auction house?" Tyler asked.

From his tone of voice, Pembroke could tell he was on the verge of crying. He leaned harder against his best friend, and they took a moment to comfort each other.

"I was injured," he said. "The owner kept me around for a bit, but even after I healed, she could see I'd lost my will to fight. I guess she decided not to waste all the money she spent buying and training me, and she sold me back."

And that was how Pembroke had ended up with Tyler. They'd quickly become friends because it was the only way to be close to someone in their situation. Pembroke didn't think he'd have survived if it hadn't been for Tyler, and now, they were both free.

If this was a dream, he never wanted to wake up.

Remington was pissed, and it took everything he had not to storm out of the kitchen.

How dare these people hurt Pembroke like that? How dare they use shifters and force them to kill each other?

He'd already been convinced that he wanted to take down the auction house and everyone involved in it, but now, he promised himself that he would, if it was the last thing he did. Those humans didn't deserve to live after what they'd done. They deserved to be thrown to the wolves and lions they'd used as pawns.

"After a while, Colbert bought me," Pembroke continued. "He knew I was damaged and never used me to fight. I was part of the security system of his mansion. I remember that he used to have me shift in front of people when they came to the house so he could boast about having a hydra protecting him. It was better than what had been done to me before. As long as I followed his orders, I was pretty much left alone, and no one hurt me. I got along with most of the other shifters who lived in the house, although not with the guards."

"You were still a prisoner," Tyler murmured.

That was true. The situation with Colbert might have been better than what he'd been through before, but he still hadn't been free, and it had taken its toll on him. It would take him a while to heal from all that, but he was strong, and Remington knew he'd get better eventually. He wasn't alone anymore. He'd have all the support he needed from Tyler and Ryland and from the pack, and he'd never be hurt again by any of these people.

"You're safe now," Remington said before he could think better of it. "The pack will keep you safe, as will your brother, and I'll make sure Colbert and his friends can never hurt you again."

Remington realized his outburst wasn't like him, and he

wasn't the only one. Everyone around the table was staring at him. Ryland's eyes were wide, while Tyler looked almost smug. Pembroke was looking at Remington like he'd hung the moon.

"I don't know how to thank you for all of this," Pembroke said.

Remington told himself he wasn't going to blush just because a pretty man was thanking him. "I was doing my job."

"I don't think you were, not entirely. You were helping Ryland because you're his friend."

Pembroke had him there. "No one deserves to go through what you've been through."

Cam cleared his throat. "Remington is right. Everyone here wants to take down the auction house, and we'll keep you and anyone else we find there safe. I know you've been through a lot, Pembroke, and you're probably not ready to make big decisions, but you'll always have a place here." Cam looked up at Ryland and Remington. "You, too. I'd like to think we've become close during our search for Pembroke, so if you ever need anything, you just need to ask, and you're always welcome here in pack territory."

Remington was surprised to be included. He understood why Ryland had been, but him? He was nothing to any of these people. Technically, neither was Ryland, but Tyler was a pack member now, and Pembroke would probably become one, too. Since Ryland was his brother, it made sense for him to be pulled into this, but Remington was just a friend.

"Toby and I would like to offer all of you guestrooms in our home for the night," Cam continued. "Tomorrow you can start thinking about what you want to do next, but Pembroke, I want you to know that you're safe here. You're surrounded by shifters, both normal and rare. We have two phoenix shifters, a griffin, and a chimera. They can protect you better than anyone else."

Pembroke looked exhausted. He nodded and continued clutching his mug as if it were a lifeline. Remington understood, even though he'd never been in Pembroke's position. He had to be overwhelmed and needed time alone to wrap his mind around everything that happened.

"We'll gladly accept your offer," Ryland said. "I think that staying here for a few days is the best thing we can do."

"I'll stay, too," Remington declared. "I'll reach out to Braden to find out what happened after we left. I'll let you know."

Things moved quickly after that. Everyone got up, and Toby and Tyler disappeared with Pembroke. Remington headed outside to call Braden, stopping on the porch so he wouldn't be far from Pembroke and Ryland. He wasn't surprised when Ryland followed him. He might not have gone through the same hell as Pembroke, but after looking for his brother for three years and wondering if he was still alive, he had to be overwhelmed, too.

"I thought you'd insist on taking him home tonight," Remington told him.

"I wanted to, but I saw how he was surrounded by other shifters. As much as I love him, I'm only human, and there are certain things I can't give him. I think he'll feel safer here, surrounded by people who can actually protect him if someone comes for him." He hesitated. "You don't think they will, do you?"

"I don't believe Colbert will be able to do anything, considering the pack took everything from him. As for the others, how can they know where he is? Even if they did, it would be foolish to attack the pack. They might not know about all the rare shifters living here, but this is still a wolf pack."

Ryland visibly relaxed. For some reason, he trusted Remington with his brother's life, and it was humbling. Remington never wanted to break that trust, which meant he'd have to stay away from Pembroke.

Ryland sighed. "I want nothing more than to lock Pembroke away so that nothing and no one can ever hurt him again, but I know that's not right. He'd start hating me, and I can't let that happen after I just got him back. I'm just terrified of what might happen to him if I lose sight of him. I feel he'll disappear again, even though I know that's not true."

"Give yourself time." Remington hated that his friend was in pain, even though it was normal and no one could do anything about it. Only time would heal Pembroke and Ryland, but it would be easier if they stayed close and listened to each other.

"I know. I just need to make sure these assholes can't ever touch him again."

"We will. You're not in this alone, Ryland. I want Pembroke safe as much as you do."

"I couldn't have asked for a better friend. I didn't know how lucky I was when I met you and Braden, but I know now. You saved my brother."

"I didn't. He saved himself while I worked to find him. The important thing is that he's all right. Don't smother him with love and attention. He needs to start living his life. It won't be easy or fast, but it doesn't need to be. He needs a good support system and people he feels safe with. Don't allow your fears to make you do something stupid."

Ryland grinned. "Even if I do something stupid, you'll be there to stop me. You're my conscience."

Remington didn't like that because of the way he felt about Pembroke. He didn't know Pembroke personally, but he'd heard so many things about him over the past three years that he felt he did. He'd always liked what Ryland told him about his brother, but now, Pembroke was right there in front of him, and he was incredibly handsome and strong, yet fragile at the same time. Ryland wanted to protect him, but

Remington? Remington wanted to get to know him and to find out the kind of person he'd become over the past three years.

He wanted to find out if the person Pembroke was now would be a good fit for him, and that scared him.

# CHAPTER THREE

Physically, Pembroke was all right. He'd had a few aches and soreness when he'd arrived in Rosewood, but they were gone now. He'd been resting for the past several days, something he hadn't been allowed to do for the past three years. He'd slept more than he could remember ever sleeping and spent a lot of time spread out on his bed and staring at the ceiling just because he could. There was no one to tell him he needed to get a move-on and stop wasting time. There was no one to yell at him that given how much they'd paid for him, he needed to earn his keep. He was just here, staring at his bedroom ceiling.

Every time he tried doing something in the house, Toby appeared to stop him. The alpha wasn't far behind, and that wasn't even considering Ryland. Pembroke was feeling coddled, and he was surprised to realize he didn't mind it that much.

Maybe he deserved to be coddled after what had happened to him. He suspected everyone around him was trying to show him how much they cared by making his life easier, and he appreciated it. It was taking his brain a little while to fully understand that he was free and needed to get back to a normal life in which he had to find a job, pay bills, and worry about what he'd get for dinner rather than whether or not he'd survive the day.

That was where the problems started. His body might have healed, but his mind was a mess.

Pembroke hadn't expected everything to magically be all

right as soon as he was away from Colbert. That wasn't how things went, no matter how much he wished they did. He still had nightmares, but he was sure he could get over those eventually. He just didn't know what to do with himself.

The first three days had been great and, at the same time, overwhelming. Ryland and Tyler had barely left Pembroke's side. They'd stuck around Cam and Toby's house, bringing him anything he might need, from food to drinks to books to distract himself. After that, things changed. Ryland still lived in the house with them, but he needed to work, so he spent a lot of time on his phone and computer. To Pembroke's surprise, Tyler had told him he now had a family. He needed to focus on them rather than Pembroke.

Pembroke still couldn't believe it. Tyler had gone from being a prisoner to having a boyfriend and a kid. Cora was Matt's daughter, but Pembroke had seen Tyler with her, and it was clear they cared about each other. Matt seemed like a nice guy, if a bit nervous, and as long as Tyler was happy, Pembroke was, too.

Everyone had something to focus on except for Pembroke. That gave him way too much time to obsess over what had happened to him, and he didn't know how to deal with any of the emotions those thoughts created. Staring at the ceiling wasn't helping, but Pembroke hadn't expected it to.

That meant something needed to change.

He sat up. He suspected that if he tried leaving the house, someone would immediately find out and insist on going with him. He didn't mind spending time with people who cared about him. He'd missed them, and it was great to finally feel part of a family again. But sometimes, they were a lot to deal with, especially Ryland. He'd gone straight into overprotective mode, and Pembroke didn't know how to deal with it.

No one had ever been overprotective when it came to him. His parents had barely cared about him, and he'd spent more time with Ryland growing up than he had with them, even though Ryland was fifteen years older. After Ryland left for college, Pembroke had grown up on his own with a nanny to watch over him. Ryland had returned as often as he could, but it hadn't felt like enough. Even after graduating from college, he'd gone on to work and build his company. Pembroke had always known that Ryland loved him, but it was a love that had worked from afar.

That wasn't so anymore. It was almost smothering in a way Pembroke hadn't expected, and he didn't know what to do about it. For the past three years especially, no one had cared if he lived or died. Now, everyone seemed to expect him to break down. Every time he so much as sniffed, they rushed to reassure him that everything would be okay and that it was normal for him to feel out of place and overwhelmed.

They were right, but that didn't mean Pembroke had to like it. He understood where they were coming from and why they behaved like this, but it was too much, which was why he was spending a lot of time in his room. The problem was that he'd been a prisoner for three years, and no matter how comfortable the room was, it felt like a cell.

Being alone was fine. Pembroke was used to it and even liked it. After three years of spending almost every moment he was awake with other people, from shifters to humans, it felt good not to have anyone watch him or to have to answer any questions. It gave him time to think about what he'd lost, what he had now, and what he could have in the future.

He had no idea.

He knew he was safe, but that was where things ended. He'd been going to college before being kidnapped, but he didn't know if he could see himself going back and getting his degree. He felt it didn't matter anymore, and the guy he'd been back then wasn't the guy he was now. He'd had dreams of getting his degree and maybe working with Ryland, but now, the only thing he could focus on was living a peaceful life. He wanted to hide in pack territory and make it so that no one would ever attempt to take him against his will again. He wanted to be with Tyler, get to know him outside the cages, and be happy.

Right now, that felt impossible.

He pushed away from his bed. He liked spending time alone, but this bedroom was starting to feel suffocating, as if the four walls were closing in on him. He needed out, but if he opened the bedroom door, someone would be there to ask him if everything was all right. They'd see that everything *wasn't* all right and try to fix it.

But they couldn't fix him.

He eyed the window. It wasn't huge, but he wasn't a big guy. He could easily fit through it. If anyone found out, they'd freak out, but he could leave a note on his pillow. He'd been given a cell phone, so he'd take it along, and anyone looking for him could call him.

Pembroke's heart raced as he neared the window. He couldn't remember the last time he'd done something like this. He wasn't disobeying an order, but it still felt like he was doing something he shouldn't. It felt good because he was finally able to do what he wanted when he wanted to do it.

And so what if he wanted to sneak out the window and run in the forest?

He yearned to explore the area around the house, and that was what he was going to do. The one time he'd left Toby's house to see where Tyler lived hadn't been enough.

He opened the window, peeking outside to make sure no one would see him. It was the middle of the day, so most people were working. That meant he'd be able to get out without anyone stopping him, which was what he wanted.

He moved back into the bedroom, grabbed a piece of paper and a pencil, and scribbled a note for Ryland that he left on his pillow. His new phone was already in his pocket, so he pushed his feet into a pair of shoes, grabbed another sweater, and climbed out of the window.

The leaves crackled under his feet when he landed. He sucked in a breath, but it wasn't an uncommon noise to hear in this kind of place, and no one came looking. He took a deep breath, then another, and he realized he was smiling.

He was free.

Pembroke wrapped the other sweater around his shoulders and moved away from the house. It was cold, but he didn't care.

For a moment, he hesitated, not knowing where to go. Tyler's house was the only other place he knew in pack territory, so he headed that way. He hoped no one would notice him until he reached it, so he stopped when he noticed a car parked in front of it. There was a woman inside. She was watching the house, and since Pembroke didn't know her, he decided he might as well watch her until she left.

He didn't have anything better to do, anyway.


Remington stared at his computer without seeing it. He was wasting time, but he didn't think he could focus.

He'd tried over the past few days. He was still staying at Cam and Toby's house, even though he'd mentioned going back home several times. Every time he did, Ryland went into a panic, as if he needed Remington there to hold his hand while he got reacquainted with his brother.

It was ridiculous. Ryland and Pembroke were adults and could do this without Remington hovering around them, especially given how Remington felt about Pembroke. Pembroke didn't need Remington drooling all over him. What he needed was time and space to heal, which was why Remington had tried his best to avoid him, even though they lived in the same house for now. He'd thought it would be nearly impossible because of that, but Pembroke barely left the bedroom he was staying in, so they'd only seen each other a few times during the meals.

Remington was worried, which was why he wasn't able to focus on his work. What was happening to Pembroke? Was this normal, or was he struggling? If he was, was there anything Remington could do to help him?

Remington snorted. If there was anyone who could do anything for Pembroke, it would be Ryland or even Tyler. Remington wasn't Pembroke's friend. He wasn't Pembroke's anything. His place wasn't here with Pembroke and Ryland but back at home, and he needed to remember that.

But he couldn't seem to leave, no matter how hard he tried to convince himself. He checked in with Braden daily, so he knew the company was fine even without him there. Braden and the people who worked for them had gone home after freeing every shifter they'd found in Colbert's mansion. There had been a few wounded, and Braden had mentioned the shifters killing several guards, but that was none of their business. They'd done what they'd been there for, and what the shifters did after that was their problem. They'd offered help, but most of those shifters didn't trust anyone, so they'd declined.

Remington didn't blame them. He'd been at the auction when Ryland had bought Tyler, and he'd seen what those people did. He didn't have to be told to know that the shifters had gone through hell, and if they wanted revenge, who was he to stop them from getting it? As far as he knew, Colbert was still hiding somewhere, trying to get to his money every so often. Angus had made sure he couldn't touch a cent of it, and the thought always made Remington smile. Maybe that made him a bad person, but he didn't care.

"Hey," Ryland said as he walked into the kitchen.

Remington smiled at him. "Taking a break?"

"Looks like you've been doing the same," Ryland teased.

Remington couldn't tell him he was distracted because if he did, he'd have to explain why he was, and that wasn't something he felt comfortable doing. How could he tell Ryland that he couldn't stop thinking about his brother?

He shrugged. "I'm used to working in my office, so this is kind of weird."

Ryland poured himself a cup of coffee and leaned a hip against the counter. "I know it was a lot of me to ask, so thanks for sticking around."

"You're one of my best friends. If you need me, I'm here." It was as simple as that, even without considering Pembroke. The fact that Remington wanted to stay to make sure he was all right hadn't influenced his decision to do as Ryland had asked.

Ryland's smile was tired, but it was there. Remington had seen him smile more often over the past few days than in the three years since they'd met, and it was all because Pembroke was back.

"How's your brother?" he asked.

Ryland took a moment to answer. "I'm not sure. He's not exactly hiding from me, but he also isn't talking to me."

"You need to give him time. He's been alone for the past three years, and I know you weren't very close even before then."

"We should have been. Maybe if we had been, he wouldn't have been taken."

"You can't blame yourself for something like that. You didn't kidnap and sell him, so it was *not* your fault. You know that, as does Pembroke. He doesn't blame you for what happened to him."

Ryland grimaced. "But I blame myself."

"And you shouldn't. If he doesn't blame you, and he's the

person who was affected by this, why should you?"

"I just want the best for him." Ryland hesitated. "And right now, I think that the best is for him to stay here with the pack. He needs to be safe and protected and be around people he can trust. This is a small town, and with the number of rare shifters in the pack, I believe this could be a home for Pembroke."

"He should be the one to decide that."

Ryland nodded slowly. "I'm not going to force him, but he's not the only reason I was thinking about that. I like it here. I think it's a great place, in the middle of the woods, with a bunch of people who feel like family. I feel better here than in my apartment in the city, and I don't want to leave."

Remington closed his laptop and looked at his friend. He'd seen Ryland more relaxed and smiling a lot, and he'd thought it was because of Pembroke, but maybe that wasn't the case. Maybe there was more to Ryland's happiness than having his brother back, although Pembroke's presence in his life was a big reason. "Are you thinking about moving here?"

"You were always able to read my mind."

"I don't read your mind. I'm observant, and I know you."

Ryland grinned. "You do. And yes, I'm thinking of moving here permanently. I think Pembroke will want to stay, and it's a good idea. Here, he'll have a strong support system and be safe without having to hide. I'm not a shifter, so I can't even begin to imagine how hard it is for a rare shifter to hide what they are, but I don't want Pembroke to have to do that. He's been through enough. He should be able to live his life the way he wants without having to look over his shoulder the entire time. Besides, Tyler is here, and he's not moving. I'm pretty sure the two of them would strangle me if I tried separating them."

He wasn't wrong. Tyler had been spending more time with Pembroke than with his boyfriend and their family. Matt didn't seem to mind, but then he'd been there when Ryland had bought Tyler at the auction. He'd had a glimpse into what life had been for Tyler and Pembroke, so it made sense that he understood they needed each other.

So Pembroke and Ryland were moving to Rosewood. Where did that leave Remington? His job was in the city with Braden. He'd been spending a lot of time in Rosewood with Ryland because of Pembroke, but that part of the job was over. Nothing was keeping him here except for his best friend, and since Ryland wasn't going back, Remington needed to make a decision. He couldn't stay here forever, hanging around the brothers.

Or could he?

He knew what he wanted, but it was dangerous. If he followed his heart, he'd move here faster than even Ryland could and would focus on Pembroke and trying to earn his trust, and then, more. He'd never push him into anything, but he couldn't help but wonder if moving was a good idea, considering how close it would bring him to Pembroke.


Pembroke had no idea who that woman was, but he watched her with interest as she left her car and went to knock on Tyler's door. Pembroke expected Tyler to open, but the house was silent, and nothing happened. Was Tyler out? He'd told Pembroke that for now, he was staying home with Cora and Matt and that there were circumstances that made it hard for either he or Matt to find a job, but he hadn't gone into details. Pembroke was curious, but since Tyler was clearly uncomfortable talking about whatever was happening, he hadn't pushed. Maybe Tyler felt that way because he thought Pembroke couldn't take it, but Pembroke could use the distraction.

Maybe those circumstances had something to do with this woman. She continued knocking on the door for what felt like forever, and when the door still didn't open, she peeked through the window next to it. She went as far as cupping her hands on the glass and leaning in to see better.

Pembroke didn't like her, probably because he felt she was a threat to his friend, but he hoped he was wrong. Maybe they had an appointment, and she'd gotten the date wrong.

Pembroke wondered who she was. He suspected she might be Cora's mother. Cora was six, and she had to have come from somewhere. It wouldn't be a surprise to find out that Cora's mother was in the picture. Even if she and Matt were divorced, Cora was still her daughter.

But there was something about the way this woman moved around the outside of the house that made Pembroke want to growl at her. He'd been hypervigilant for the past three years and had seen the worst humanity had to offer. He knew how much human beings could hurt other humans and shifters, and his instincts had always been spot on.

He knew they were this time, too, when the woman finally turned.

Pembroke hadn't seen her face until now. He was hidden in the forest at a distance behind the car. He'd been able to see the woman in the car and when she got out, but she'd never turned. She'd been focused on the house, while Pembroke had been focused on her. Maybe she'd caught his attention because she felt familiar, but he hadn't realized that until she turned.

He recognized her.

Every single human involved in the auctions was a bad person. The guards knew what they were paid to do, and they knew that as long as they didn't hurt the merchandise and leave permanent marks, the owner wouldn't care what they did. Fulton, the man in charge of the operation, was a special brand of evil. He was the one who sold and bought shifters, and he saw them as nothing more than animals. He used them to make himself rich and didn't care what happened to them.

Then, there was his fiancée, Pamela. Pembroke hadn't thought he'd see her again, but there she was, standing next to her car. She'd taken a phone out of her purse and had it raised to her ear, so Pembroke forced himself to stay where he was and listen to her phone call. Every fiber of his being was screaming at him to grab her and stomp on her until she was nothing more than a bloody pancake, but he had questions.

Why was she in pack territory? Why was she knocking on Tyler's door? Even worse, why hadn't anyone stopped her? Tyler had to have recognized her if he'd seen her before, which would explain why he hadn't opened the door.

There was no way she was here to get Tyler and Pembroke back. She was only one human woman. She couldn't convince them to follow her, no matter how many times she threatened them. Besides, Cam and Toby had promised Pembroke that he was safe, and from what little Pembroke had seen of them, they weren't liars. Without a good reason, they wouldn't allow a woman like Pamela to waltz in and out of pack territory.

If Tyler had recognized her, he'd told Cam and Toby about it. They had to know who Pamela was and that she was in pack territory, yet they hadn't done anything to stop her.

What was going on?

"No one is opening the door," Pamela said.

Pembroke turned his attention back to her. She seemed agitated and angry, and she kept glancing at the door of the house in which Tyler lived.

"Of course I tried more than once. Do you take me for an idiot?" she snapped. "They're not going to open. That asshole isn't going to let me in."

*That asshole* could only be Tyler. Pembroke was confused. If Tyler had recognized Pamela, why was she allowed in pack territory?

"They both know I don't care about Cora and that I'm here

for something else," Pamela insisted. "I don't know why you thought this was going to work. Tyler told everyone who I was, including Matt. What do you expect me to do when no one opens the door?"

Pembroke wished he could hear the other side of the conversation. He suspected Pamela was talking to Fulton, and he was as confused as her. Why would Tyler and Matt open their door for her? And what did Cora have to do with this? Was she Cora's mother like Pembroke had thought earlier? But even if she was, there was no way Tyler would allow her anywhere near the girl. She had to know that, so why was she here?

"I want him to be the first to pay," Pamela spat out. "You can promise me that, can't you? He and Matt will be the first to go, and that brat will be right after them."

Pembroke's stomach churned. He'd always known Pamela was evil. Only an evil person would work with Fulton and get engaged to him, and he'd seen Pamela walking around the auction house. She knew what happened there, and she didn't care.

Part of Pembroke suspected she liked it. Buying and selling shifters enabled her to buy fancy clothes and shoes, and she probably wouldn't have cared even if Fulton had been selling humans instead of shifters. She didn't have a conscience. Her heart was black as coal, and eventually, she'd pay for what she'd done. She might not have started the auction house, but she worked there and deserved everything terrible that would ever happen to her.

"Well, I'm leaving. They're not going to open, anyway. No, I'm not going to walk around the forest in these shoes. What did you expect anyway? For a fucking phoenix to land in front of me? Tyler probably told everyone who I am, and they'll never trust me."

She hung up and climbed into her car. Pembroke watched

as she drove away, but even after he couldn't see the car anymore, he stayed where he was. He was terrified that she was going to come back, and if she did, there was a chance she'd take him away.

Just the thought freaked him out. He didn't want to be a prisoner anymore. He didn't want to be sold like a piece of meat.

The front door creaked open, and Tyler's head popped out. He looked down the driveway, and even from a distance, Pembroke could see the moment he realized Pamela was gone and relaxed. He disappeared back inside and started closing the door, so Pembroke rushed forward.

"Tyler!" he called out.

Tyler's eyes widened, and he stepped onto the porch. "Pembroke? What are you doing here?"

"I wanted to see you."

"You could have called. I would have come to you."

Pembroke glared at him and climbed the porch steps. "I can walk, and I wanted to. I love that Cam and Toby took me under their wings, but I can't stay in their guestroom forever doing nothing."

"You just arrived?"

It sounded like Tyler was afraid that Pembroke had seen Pamela. Pembroke didn't think he wanted to hide this from him, but rather that he wanted to shield him from what was happening.

He came to stop in front of his friend. "I've been here for a while but was hiding in the forest. I saw her, Tyler."

Tyler briefly closed his eyes. "I'd hoped you hadn't."

"What is she doing here? Why is she allowed to come in and out of pack territory? Cam promised we were safe."

"We *are* safe."

"Not if she's here. Don't you remember what she did to us?"

"I remember all too well, but we don't have a choice." Tyler stepped to the side and gestured at Pembroke to come in. "She's Cora's mother, and you know how much money she has. She's threatened Matt to take Cora away, and even though we have a lawyer, she might be able to. Cam knows who she is and what she did, and he and the others are keeping an eye on her, but we want to find out what she's doing here and what she actually wants, and we won't be able to do so if we don't allow her in pack territory."

Pembroke had been right, and he wished he hadn't been.

***Remington had finally managed to focus on his work after talking to Ryland. He was glad to know that his friend was taking things with Pembroke one day at a time, as he should. It would be useless to push Pembroke into making decisions, especially decisions that would change his life. Pembroke needed time, and even though Ryland was excited to have his brother back, he seemed to understand that.

Remington wasn't surprised that Ryland would be moving here. He'd suspected Pembroke would become a pack member, and Ryland had been looking for his brother for too long. He blamed himself for what had happened and wanted to be as close to Pembroke as possible.

Remington didn't know where that left him, but he'd find out eventually. It wasn't like he'd lose his friend if Ryland moved. Even if they were far from each other, they could use phones and email to communicate.

Ryland moving didn't mean Remington had to move, too.

He huffed at the way he'd allowed his mind to get distracted again and turned his attention back to his computer screen. He had several new requests for jobs. He needed to go over all of them, decide which ones the company would accept, and assign people to them. It wasn't his favorite part of the job, but it needed to be done, and he wasn't doing anything else, anyway.

He heard the front door open, swore because it was yet another distraction, and looked up at the sound of footsteps coming toward the kitchen. It wasn't unheard of for people to be coming and going. This was the alpha's house, and pack members were always welcome. It wasn't a bad thing, but sometimes, it could be a bother, like today. Remington hoped no one needed him because he was busy.

But the two men who appeared at the kitchen door made him close his laptop. He hadn't expected Pembroke to be with Tyler. The last time he'd checked, Pembroke had been in his room. Remington hadn't heard him open the front door, and they had come in together.

"Where are you two coming from?" he asked.

Tyler flopped into one of the chairs. "My house. Pamela came back."

There were two things there that Remington wanted to focus on. "How did Pembroke get to your house?"

"Pembroke is right here, so you could ask him," Pembroke grumbled.

He stayed on his feet behind Tyler, and Remington didn't miss the way he was touching Tyler's shoulder as if to reassure him. That would make sense since Tyler had said that Pamela had come back.

"You were in your bedroom," Remington told Pembroke.

"Until I had enough and climbed out the window. That's not the important thing here. Can you focus on Pamela?"

Remington didn't want to, but he should. It was the only way to protect the two men in front of him.

He looked at Tyler. "What happened?"

"She knocked on the door, but I didn't answer. I saw her peeking through the windows, too, but I was near the top of the stairs, and she didn't see me. I don't know what she wanted, but I imagine it has something to do with Cora. She's still threatening to take her back."

"She can't do that, can she?" Pembroke asked.

Tyler looked up at him. "The lawyer said that she couldn't. She abandoned her two sons with Matt, then Cora when she was born, and Matt raised all three of them. Even though he's not Cora's biological father, there's no way anyone will give Cora to Pamela. She was never in her daughter's life, and Cora doesn't know her."

Remington had already heard this explanation. He also knew why Cam had allowed Pamela to continue coming and going. "You didn't talk to her?"

Tyler shook his head. "I didn't want to."

"I heard her speaking on the phone," Pembroke said. "She was telling someone that no one had opened and that they wouldn't. She sounded angry."

Remington nodded. "All right. I'll tell Cam and the others about this, but I don't think you need to worry, Tyler. As long as you don't let her in and don't talk to her, there's little she can do."

"I wish I could believe that," Tyler muttered.

He got to his feet and turned to Pembroke. "I'm going home. No more going out the window, all right? If you want to visit, just call me. I don't want anything to happen to you."

"I wouldn't have snuck out the window if someone had told me I might find Pamela waiting for me outside," Pembroke argued.

"Well, now you know, so you'll stay here."

Pembroke looked miffed, but he nodded. It was good that Tyler could get him to agree to this because if he hadn't, Remington would have had to follow Pembroke around, and he doubted Pembroke would have enjoyed it.

He wanted freedom, which was understandable. After being in a cage for so long, he deserved to be free and allowed to go anywhere he wanted without having to fear that someone would attack him.

The problem was the reality they were dealing with. Even though Tyler and Pembroke were free, Pamela and Fulton were still working at the auction house. They wouldn't hesitate to snatch them if they could get their hands on them, which meant Pembroke needed to be careful.

"Everyone swore to me that I'd be safe here," Pembroke said.

Remington's heart broke for him. "You are," he said. "We'll keep you safe, and we're not saying you can't leave the house, just to be careful. It's not like Pamela spends every day here. She comes around a couple times a week to threaten Matt, but that's it."

Tyler snorted. "Glad to hear you don't think that's bad."

"You know that's not what I think."

Tyler sighed. "Fine. I'm going home. Cora will be back soon, and I don't want her to freak out if she doesn't find anyone there. You need to be careful, Pembroke. I know this isn't what you hoped for, but I trust Remington and the others to keep us safe. I even trust them to keep Cora and Matt safe."

Pembroke still looked angry, but he hugged Tyler. Tyler nodded at Remington as he left, and when Remington heard the front door open and close, he realized he and Pembroke were alone together.

He didn't know what to say. He didn't want to spook Pembroke, who was already angry. It was probably better if he went back to work, but what if Pembroke needed comfort?

Pembroke moved closer to Remington and looked up at him. "You'll keep me safe?"

Remington nodded. "I swear I will."

"Why? Is my brother paying you?"

"Not anymore. I'm doing this because he's my best friend and because you deserve to live your life without fear."

"I don't think it's going to happen anytime soon."

"You'll get there," Remington promised.

Pembroke stared at him. "There's something about you," he finally said.

Remington's heart beat faster. "Is there?"

Remington had no idea what that meant or what Pembroke was doing. He didn't stop him when he moved even closer, though, or when he hooked his hands behind Remington's neck. Remington also didn't stop him when he kissed him.

The kiss wasn't deep. It was barely more than a press of their lips, but it was enough to give Remington a taste of Pembroke, and even that was enough to know he needed more.

He didn't take it. If anything was going to happen between them, Pembroke would have to take those steps. He had with the kiss, but maybe that was all he wanted.

Pembroke didn't let go of Remington. Remington stared at him, wondering what had just happened. "Why did you do that?" he asked in a husky voice he barely recognized.

"Because I wanted to. I want normalcy, Remington. I want to get my own place, find a job, and be in a relationship."

Remington made a strangled sound. "With me?"

Pembroke smiled. "I don't know who to trust, but if Ryland trusts you, that means I can, too. You were there when I was rescued, so you know how messed up I am, and you're not too bad to look at."

Remington laughed. "You're not making me feel great."

"Well, you *should* feel great. After everything that happened to me, I trust *you*."

That was all Remington cared about. Well, that and the fact that since Pembroke had come close enough that Remington could smell it, Remington could tell they were mates.

# CHAPTER FOUR

Pembroke was back in the cage, and nothing changed, no matter how much he begged or tried to pull at the bars. He couldn't see anything else in the room around him. Everything was white, and he was alone.

*Completely alone.*

*There was no Tyler, no Ryland, and certainly no Remington. It was just white and fear, and as Pembroke screamed, he knew no one would come for him.*

Pembroke jerked into a sitting position in his bed. His eyes were wide, and he was sweating. His heart raced as his body got ready to run. The sheets were tangled around his legs, trapping him. He panted while he quickly worked to untangle them in case he needed to be able to run.

He didn't. He wasn't in a cage. He was in his bed in Rosewood, and he was still free.

Physically, anyway.

He flopped back against the pillow. Even though it was dark, he could vaguely see the ceiling. Staring at it gave his body time to come down from the panic that had gripped it, and he forced himself to breathe in and out as slowly as he could. He wasn't in danger and hadn't been, even though his nightmare had told him the opposite. It had only been a dream, and Pembroke needed to remember that.

He did remember it, but that didn't mean it was easy to deal with. He sucked in a breath, then another, and when his heart finally slowed down, he sat up again. He needed a shower but didn't know if he had the strength to get out of bed.

The problem was that he wouldn't be able to sleep again. He was still freaking out, and nothing but time would change that. Even though his brain knew that nothing had happened, his fear was strong enough that he had to resist the urge to run.

Where would he go, anyway? This was the safest place for him. He was surrounded by shifters who'd made it their duty to save rare shifters from the people hurting them. Even more importantly, he was surrounded by people who cared about him. His brother, Tyler, and Remington wouldn't ever allow anyone to hurt him again. Cam and Toby would defend him, too. They barely knew him, yet they'd welcomed him into their home and their lives. He wasn't a pack member yet, but he knew that if he asked, he'd be welcomed as one.

With a huff, he got out of bed. He shivered in the cool night air. The sweat was still drying on his body, and he felt icky, so he headed to the bathroom.

He felt better once he was clean and dressed in warm clothes, but trying to get more sleep would be useless. Just the thought of stretching out on the bed and staring at the ceiling again made his skin itch. He needed to find something else to do. He could stay in his room and try to distract himself with a book or a TV show, but once again, the four walls felt like they were closing in on him.

He needed out.

He'd promised Remington he wouldn't sneak out the window again, so after putting on shoes and a jacket, he headed toward the door. He left a note on his pillow, even though the first time, no one had found it. He didn't want anyone to freak out if they realized he was gone.

The house was silent as he made his way through it. It was four AM, so no one would wake up for a while. Maybe it would be long enough for Pembroke to take a walk in the forest and come back. If anyone realized he'd had a nightmare, they'd want to talk about it, and that was the last thing he wished for.

He already knew what the nightmares meant. They were happening because of what he'd been through, and he would never be able to forget the past three years. Maybe the nightmares would stop in time, but in the meantime, Pembroke could deal with them on his own.

The air was colder outside the house, but it wasn't raining or snowing. Pembroke could see his breath in front of his face as he quickly walked toward the trees. Most people would be afraid of walking in the forest during the night, especially alone, but he wasn't. He was in a safe place, and if his path crossed with someone else's, he could shift into his hydra form and defend himself. Knowing that felt good, especially because in the rest of his life, he let other people defend him.

He needed to stop being so afraid of Pamela and Fulton. The first time, they'd taken him by surprise. He'd been in college and hadn't shifted because he'd been terrified someone would see him. He wouldn't make that mistake twice. He wasn't in a cage anymore, and as long as he could avoid being put in one again, he would stay free.

But he didn't want to shift if he could avoid it. He'd been forced to spend so much time in his hydra form that he didn't want to do so again for a while. That had been the only form useful to Colbert, and even though the hydra was part of him, in a way, he hated it.

He'd been taken because he was a hydra shifter. That was why he'd been forced to fight to the death and hurt people, then to defend Colbert's home. None of that would have happened if he'd been a mouse shifter or something. He couldn't change what he was, but he could avoid it for a little while. He'd spent three years being forced to stay in one form or the other depending on where he was and who had bought him.

Now, *he* was the one who decided what he wanted to be.

The sound of a branch cracking high above his head made him stop. He looked up and squinted, but he couldn't see anything in the darkness. He started walking again, but he could still hear noises, and he felt as if someone was watching him.

He was ready to shift, but he didn't need to. Two wide wings appeared, and Tyler landed in front of him.

Pembroke pressed a hand against his chest. "You scared me."

"I'm sorry. I didn't mean to, but I wasn't sure it was you. What are you doing here in the middle of the night?"

Pembroke arched a brow. "I could ask you the same thing."

A white bird flew down and landed on Tyler's shoulder. It looked like a pigeon, but it was dark, so Pembroke could be wrong.

"I couldn't sleep, and neither could Peregrine," Tyler explained. "We often meet during the night when we have nightmares."

So the white bird was Peregrine and clearly a shifter. "I couldn't sleep either."

Tyler nodded as if he understood, and he probably did. He'd been in those cages, too. They hadn't really talked about what had happened to them when they hadn't been together, but it couldn't have been pleasant. Maybe Tyler hadn't been forced to kill anyone, but it didn't mean he'd been happy with what he was forced to do.

The bird hopped off Tyler's shoulder and shifted. The blond man who appeared shivered and crouched at the base of a tree, and Pembroke realized that there was a bundle of clothes there. The man quickly put them on, and once he was dressed and wearing a heavy jacket, he turned to him.

"I'm Peregrine," he said.

Pembroke nodded. "Pembroke."

"Tyler told me about you. It's nice to meet you."

Pembroke had wanted to be alone, but this wasn't bad. "What kind of shifter are you?"

"A caladrius. I can heal illnesses. Unicorns are into wounds, while I'm into sickness."

"I don't think I've ever heard about that kind of shifter."

Peregrine shrugged. "I'd never heard about a gargoyle shifter, yet Tyler's right there. So, Tyler told me you got yourself a boyfriend?"

Pembroke turned wide eyes to Tyler, who had the good taste to look sheepish.

"I didn't say he had a boyfriend," Tyler muttered.

Peregrine waved his words away. "Doesn't matter. Why don't you tell us about him? I can tell you about my guy if you want."

Pembroke had no idea what was going on. "Remington isn't my boyfriend." He was Pembroke's mate, but Pembroke was still trying to wrap his mind around that.

"He's your *something*. Come on, Pem. You, me, and Tyler are new here. The auction assholes might not have captured me, but I've been through hell before finding this place. Now that I have, I want friends, and you're it."

Pembroke snickered. "It sounds like you're forcing me and Tyler to be your friends."

"I won't have to force you if you do it willingly." Peregrine wiggled his eyebrows.

Pembroke couldn't stop smiling. He didn't know what to think of Peregrine, but he liked him.

Peregrine and Tyler could understand what Pembroke was going through. They'd been in similar situations, but now, they were free and happy, and Pembroke wanted the same.

Maybe they could give him tips, because he had no idea how to do it.

Remington always woke up early, and today wasn't any different. He opened his eyes just before five AM, stretched, and slowly got out of bed. He liked this time of the day. The house was quiet, and he was alone, something that seldom happened during the day. Even Ryland was still sleeping, which meant Remington had a little time to himself.

He showered and dressed, then headed to the kitchen to get coffee. He hadn't stopped thinking about Pembroke since their kiss a few days ago. Pembroke hadn't exactly run away from him after kissing him, but he'd started talking about Pamela and Fulton, and it had been clear he needed time to wrap his mind around what he'd done. Remington had been happy to give him that time. He'd needed it, too, but even a few days later, he was still sure of one thing.

He wanted to kiss Pembroke again.

He was conflicted. Pembroke was an adult and his own person. He'd been through a lot, but that didn't mean anyone was allowed to take away his free will. If he wanted Remington, then he could have him because Remington wanted him, too.

But on the other hand, there was Ryland. Remington had seen how much his friend tortured himself over his brother's disappearance, so he understood why Ryland was smothering Pembroke so badly. He was terrified that if Pembroke was out of his sight, he'd be taken again. He knew that Pembroke was an adult, but he was so scared to lose him again that he was ready to lock him up to keep him safe. He wouldn't be happy when he found out that Remington and Pembroke were together.

Not that they were. They hadn't even talked about it being a possibility yet.

Remington filled a cup with coffee and leaned back against the counter to sip it. He listened to the silence in the house and closed his eyes, taking a deep breath and releasing it.

Whatever was happening with Pembroke, they'd work through it. Maybe Pembroke just wanted to be close to someone, or maybe he actually wanted Remington. Remington didn't think he'd be able to stay away from Pembroke, which meant that, eventually, he'd have to face Ryland. He wasn't looking forward to it, but Ryland needed to understand that keeping his brother safe didn't mean locking him away. He had to allow him to do what he wanted.

Remington hoped Pembroke wanted him.

He put down his mug and got another one ready. He knew that Pembroke didn't get a lot of sleep. He'd heard him have nightmares, and he ached to soothe him every time it happened. He didn't know how to do so, but maybe if Pembroke was awake, they could sit together, talk, or listen to the silence.

There was light under Pembroke's door, but when Remington knocked, no one answered. Maybe Pembroke had fallen asleep again. Remington knocked one last time, then slowly opened the door. If Pembroke was asleep, he'd turn off the light.

The bed was empty. The window was closed, so Remington didn't think Pembroke had snuck out from there, but there was no one in the bedroom or the bathroom. The shower had been recently used, though, and from the state of the bed, Remington suspected that Pembroke had a nightmare. It looked like once he'd woken up, he'd showered and headed out.

Which meant he was in the forest, alone in the dark.

He'd probably be fine, but Remington needed to make sure. He doubted Fulton and Pamela would visit pack territory at this hour of the morning, but the thought that they might made him panic. Pembroke was more than capable of defending himself, but what if they took him by surprise? What if he didn't see them coming?

Remington was already dressed, so it only took him a few moments to put on shoes and a jacket. He tried to stay as quiet as he could as he closed the front door, and once outside, he raised his head and sniffed. He could shift into his lion form, but if Pembroke needed help, Remington would have to shift back, and he'd be naked in the cold. It was better as a human. He'd shift if he couldn't find Pembroke.

Since Pembroke didn't know much of pack territory, Remington thought he might have gone to Tyler's house, so that was where he headed. He was ready to walk until he reached the house, even though it was really fucking dark, but he didn't have to.

He heard someone swearing and arched a brow. That was some creative swearing, and he wondered if Pembroke would tell him where he'd learned it.

"I can't believe this," Pembroke muttered. "I survived fights with dragons, but a damn root hurt me? What the fuck?"

Remington rushed in the direction from which Pembroke's voice came. He had to suppress a smile when he finally found him leaning against a tree and glaring down at its roots. He was holding one foot up as if putting it down hurt.

"Pembroke?" Remington called out before reaching him.

Pembroke's head snapped toward him. "Remington?"

Remington was relieved to have found Pembroke. That was the only thing that mattered. "What happened?"

"Nothing."

"I heard you talking to that root."

Pembroke looked away. "I stumbled and hurt my ankle, but I'm fine. I can walk home."

"I'm sure you can, but it doesn't mean you have to." Pembroke couldn't really expect Remington to go home and leave him here knowing that his ankle hurt, right?

Pembroke sighed. "Fine. You can help me."

"Can I carry you, or do you want me to help you hop along?"

Pembroke was silent for a moment. Remington was glad he'd given him the option. Carrying Pembroke would be faster, but Remington wouldn't force him into anything he didn't want. If he wanted to hop home, he'd make sure he didn't fall on his face.

"You can carry me. I'm cold and hungry, and I want to go home."

Remington moved quickly but not so quickly that he'd scare Pembroke. He let Pembroke lean against him, and once he was sure he wouldn't spook him, he leaned down and hauled him into his arms.

"I feel like a bride," Pembroke said in a snarky tone.

"Unfortunately, we're not married."

"Unfortunately?"

*Shit.* Remington didn't want to push Pembroke into anything, not even a relationship with him. That didn't mean he didn't want one, but he had to be careful with how he spoke. "I like you," he said honestly. "I thought that was obvious."

Pembroke didn't answer. He seemed lost in his thoughts, and Remington was happy to leave him to them. He was curious, though. "What were you doing out here at five in the morning?"

"I couldn't sleep, so I decided to take a walk and found Tyler and Peregrine hanging around. We talked for a bit."

So he hadn't been alone. It was a relief. "They headed home?"

"Yeah, or I would have asked one of them to help me. I didn't expect you to be around so early."

"I saw light under your door and brought you a cup of coffee, but you weren't there."

"You went into my bedroom?"

Remington decided that honesty would be the best way to

go, even though it might mean that Pembroke would be angry at him. "I did. I knocked, but you didn't answer, and I wanted to make sure you were all right. I apologize, but I only peeked into the bedroom and the bathroom."

The house was in sight now, so Remington walked faster. It was cold, and he didn't want Pembroke to get sick.

"It's fine. It's my bedroom, but it's not like I have many things in there."

"It's still a private place for you, and I wouldn't have gone in if I hadn't been worried."

"You don't have to be worried. I'm fine."

"I know, but it doesn't mean I don't worry. Your brother is the same. He knows you're fine and can see it, but it doesn't mean he's not anxious."

"I guess I would be, too, if our roles were reversed."

They fell silent as they reached the house. Everyone still seemed to be asleep, so Remington was as quiet as possible as he took Pembroke to Pembroke's bedroom. He set him down at the door, but when he started to step away, Pembroke didn't let go.


Pembroke had no idea what he was doing, but he didn't want Remington to leave. How could he ask for that?

He didn't have a lot of experience when it came to relation-ships. He'd been twenty-two when he'd been kidnapped, and he'd only had a few boyfriends, none of them serious. They'd all been around his age, but Remington was older and wouldn't want what a twenty-year-old kid wanted. That was what Pembroke had experience with, so this was all new. Add to it the fact that Remington was Ryland's best friend, and this was a recipe for disaster, even with the mate bond between them.

Pembroke didn't care. He wanted something good,

something for himself, and he liked Remington. He was one of the few people Pembroke felt safe with, but that wasn't the only reason Pembroke wanted him. It felt like the only person who didn't look at him like he was weak and needed to be protected was Remington. He wasn't trying to hide Pembroke from the world like Ryland. He wasn't terrified every time Pembroke wanted to leave the house.

He was Pembroke's mate.

Pembroke knew how his brother would have reacted if he'd been the one to find him in the forest with a twisted ankle. He'd have freaked out, told him he shouldn't have gone out on his own, and asked him if he could do anything. He'd have tried to be gentle and understanding, but he'd have been terrified.

But Remington wasn't like that. Even though Pembroke could tell Remington cared about him, it was a different kind of affection. Remington hadn't known him until he and the others had rescued him from Colbert. Ryland might have told Remington about him, but he wouldn't feel the need to protect him as strongly as Ryland did. Pembroke liked that Remington cared about him but wasn't smothering him, and he found Remington incredibly handsome. Who wouldn't want to be with him? Remington knew what Pembroke had gone through, but he allowed him to make his own decisions and mistakes.

So Pembroke kissed Remington. He'd been the one to initiate the last time, too, and he suspected it was because Remington wanted him to feel like he was in control. For now, that was okay, but Pembroke hoped things wouldn't always be that way. He wanted Remington to take what he needed, too.

They kissed gently in the middle of the hallway, with the house silent and asleep around them. Someone was bound to wake up soon, but for now, it felt like they were the only people left in the world.

"Come in," Pembroke said. He didn't know what he was ready for but didn't want Remington to go yet.

Remington took a step back. He didn't let go of Pembroke, and Pembroke enjoyed the feeling of his hands on his hips, but he'd put distance between them, which couldn't be good.

"I want to," Remington said.

Pembroke's stomach dropped. "But you won't."

"I can't help but feel guilty about not talking to Ryland about this first."

Pembroke pushed away, but he'd forgotten that he'd hurt his ankle, so he stumbled. Remington was there to catch him, and Pembroke had to force himself not to push him away again. He didn't want to fall on his face. That would be the worst way to end this conversation, even though he desperately wanted it to be over.

"Why would you feel guilty? He doesn't control me or who I kiss," he snapped.

"I never said he controlled you, and I don't think he feels the need to control you. But he's my best friend."

"And I'm his brother, so what? You know, I never understood this kind of thing. Why wouldn't you want your best friend and your brother to be together? If you're so close to him, it means he likes and trusts you, right? So what's the problem with you and I being together?"

Remington peered into the hallway. For a moment, Pembroke thought he was about to leave, and even though they were fighting, he didn't want him to. He didn't want to be alone and wanted more time with Remington.

So what if Remington didn't want a relationship with him? Getting kisses would be worth it. It didn't matter that Pembroke wanted more. Even though he was angry, he *did* understand where Remington was coming from and why he was hesitant.

Maybe Remington was hiding behind Ryland. It was an obvious and easy excuse. If he didn't want to be with Pembroke and didn't want to hurt him, he had to find a good excuse.

Why would Remington want to be with Pembroke? Remington was Ryland's age, which meant there were about fifteen years between him and Pembroke. He had a good job, had built his own company from the ground, and lived life with a certainty Pembroke was jealous of. It seemed like Remington knew what he wanted and did what he needed to get it.

Pembroke didn't even know where to start. He didn't want to go back to college, and he didn't want to leave pack territory, but where did that leave him? He wasn't weak, but he was lost, and it was clear that he and Remington were at two different points in their lives.

He looked down at his feet. "You don't have to lie to me. Just tell me you don't want me and go." Even though they were mates, he wouldn't be surprised. He was scarred and somewhat broken.

To Pembroke's surprise, instead of doing that, Remington cupped his cheek. He stroked his thumb on Pembroke's cheekbone, and Pembroke had to look up. What was Remington thinking? What did he want?

"I never said I don't want you."

"You act like you don't."

Remington shook his head. "That's not true."

He stepped away, so Pembroke thought he was leaving, and he limped into his room. Instead, Remington followed him in and pushed the door shut. He didn't close it all the way, as if he wanted Pembroke to know he had a way out if he needed it, but it was enough to give them privacy.

Pembroke swallowed. He didn't know what was going on, and he was afraid to find out.

"I do want you, much more than I ever expected to want

anyone," Remington explained. "I feel it doesn't make sense because I barely know you, but at the same time, I know you better than a lot of people, and you're my mate. Your brother told me so many stories about you, both about when you were a child and when you went to college. He's proud of you, and he loves you deeply. You're the reason Ryland and I grew close, and I saw how destroyed Ryland was over the past three years. He did his best to go on because he wanted everything to be perfect when you came back, but these past years were hard on him, even though they weren't as hard on him as they were on you."

"It's not a competition," Pembroke muttered. "It doesn't matter who had it worse."

"You're right. I just wanted you to understand what I'm saying. In the end, what he thinks of us being together doesn't matter. You're right when you say that you're an adult who can make your own decisions and should be allowed to make them. I won't take that away from you, and if Ryland decides he doesn't want us together, it'll hurt, but as long as you and I want this, that won't matter. I just don't want us to do this the wrong way. How will he react if he finds out we lied to him? Even if he doesn't care that we're together, he'll be hurt, and it won't be the best start for a relationship between us."

Pembroke wanted to yell that it wasn't fair, but he understood what Remington was saying. No matter how much he wanted this, he didn't want to hurt his brother.

Where did that leave him?


Remington needed Pembroke to understand. He didn't want to lose either of the brothers, but if he had to choose, he'd always choose Pembroke.

It wasn't that he didn't love Ryland. He just thought that if Ryland decided to forbid him and Pembroke to be together, it would be wrong, and not just because they were mates. Pembroke deserved to be free and loved, and if he felt he could have that with Remington, Remington wasn't going to say no. He already liked him more than he should, so falling for him wouldn't take much. Losing his best friend wasn't something Remington was looking forward to, but he'd go through it if he had to.

But if he wanted a chance not to lose Ryland, he and Pembroke needed to do this the right way. That meant not hiding that they were together and being honest with Ryland from the beginning. No matter how much Remington wanted Pembroke, he wouldn't do anything with him this morning. Pembroke deserved to be loved openly, not to be hidden away.

Pembroke sighed and went to sit on his bed. He hobbled a bit on his way there, and Remington hovered close, but he didn't help him. If Pembroke needed him, he knew he was here.

It was hard to resist the urge to help. Remington wanted to protect Pembroke, just like Ryland did. The difference between them was that Remington could see that sometimes Pembroke needed to do things on his own. He could always ask for help, but it was better if Remington didn't try to give it to him if he didn't need it.

"Do you think Ryland will try to get us to stop seeing each other?" Pembroke asked.

Remington couldn't be sure, but he knew what he hoped for. "I think he'll be shocked and confused, maybe even angry because he sees you as a fragile young adult easily taken advantage of."

Pembroke scowled. "I'm not. I'm twenty-five, and I know what I'm doing."

"I never said otherwise. But Ryland remembers you as a twenty-two-year-old kid in college. Even ignoring what you've been through, a three-year difference is a lot. It will take him some time to wrap his mind around that and accept that you grew up away from him and had to deal with what was happening around you. I think he believes that if he gives you everything you need, you might be able to forget what happened to you."

"I'll never forget," Pembroke whispered.

"Ryland knows that. He just wants to make life perfect for you, and he doesn't know how to do that. That's why he's overprotective. It's his way to make you happy."

"Can't he see that I'm not happy?"

"Maybe he can, but he doesn't know what else to do. You should talk to him."

Pembroke stared at Remington. "And if I talk to him, can we be together?"

Remington wanted to say yes right away, but he had questions. This relationship was growing in an odd situation, and he felt they needed to talk and be honest if they didn't want to lose everything. "I don't understand why you're so interested in me beyond the mate bond." Was that all there was to it?

"How could I not be? You're strong but gentle. You were there for me when I needed someone and saw what I've been through, but you're not treating me like a child. My brother trusts you, which means I can do the same even though I don't know you well. You're also sexy as hell, which is a nice bonus."

Remington wasn't going to blush like a teenager, dammit. "So you want someone you feel you can trust?"

"That's not what I said. It's one of the reasons I like you, but not the only one. Don't put words in my mouth, Remington. I don't want you to treat me like I'm a stupid kid who doesn't know what he's doing."

"I apologize if that's how I made you feel."

Pembroke sighed. "I'm more sensitive than I was before

about these things. I apologize, too." He hesitated. "Do you have to go to work?"

"Not right away. It's still early."

"Would you mind getting into bed with me? Not to do anything, just to sleep. I had a nightmare, and I'd feel safer if you were with me."

How could Remington say no to that?

He couldn't.

He didn't know what would happen between him and Pembroke or what Ryland's reaction would be, but right now, Pembroke needed him. As much as Remington loved Ryland, Pembroke was the brother who was the most important to him. He wasn't sure how or why it happened, but he didn't care.

They both carefully looked away from the other as they got ready for bed. Remington couldn't stay long, but it was only five-thirty, so it would be at least an hour before anyone noticed he wasn't in his room or in the kitchen. Hopefully, that someone wouldn't be Ryland.

Remington wanted to talk to him, but he couldn't do so now, and what Pembroke wanted was more important. He and Pembroke needed to talk about what came next and how they'd talk to Ryland, but not now. Pembroke wanted to be soothed and comforted, and Remington was ready to do just that.

He kept his jeans and sweater on, but Pembroke stripped down to a t-shirt and his boxer briefs. His ankle seemed okay from a distance, but Remington wanted to give it a better look, so when Pembroke climbed onto the bed, Remington caught his leg and knelt on the floor next to it. Pembroke's cheeks went red, but he allowed Remington to move his foot this way and that and poke at it.

"Does it hurt?" Remington asked.

"A bit, but I don't think it's too bad."

"I'll keep an eye on it in case it swells, but I think you just twisted it. You should be fine walking on it later today. Just be careful, and maybe you don't go traipsing in the woods in the dark."

Pembroke snickered. It felt good to hear him laugh, and Remington felt a bit smug that he'd managed to do that. He wanted to make Pembroke smile and laugh every day, and the strength of that emotion scared him.

He'd never believed in love at first sight, and he wasn't sure this *was* love at first sight, but it felt like it because of their bond. He wanted to protect Pembroke, but he also wanted to make him happy.

He wanted them to be happy together.

He could see a future with Pembroke, which also scared him. His priority had always been his job, and after becoming friends with Ryland, finding Pembroke. Now that he'd found Pembroke, he felt a bit lost, but he knew he'd find something else to focus on soon enough.

Like the way Pembroke felt in his arms.

They settled into bed, and it felt like the most natural thing in the world. Remington was on his back with his arm around Pembroke's shoulders, holding him close as Pembroke snuggled against him. He hooked an arm around Remington's waist, then a leg over one of his.

They fit together like they were made for each other. Thinking that made Remington feel like an idiot, but he couldn't deny that was how he felt.

Even if he and Pembroke didn't work out, he'd always be there for him. He'd keep him safe from afar, and if Pembroke ever needed him, he'd be there. If Pembroke only wanted Remington to protect him, that was what he'd do.

Remington wanted so much he couldn't put it into words. It could mean the end of his friendship with Ryland, but he prayed that wouldn't be the case.

He didn't want to lose either of the brothers. He wanted to protect both of them, and as long as they allowed him to, he would.

But he also wanted to love Pembroke.

# CHAPTER FIVE

"You're smiling."

Tyler's words caused Pembroke to smile even wider. "Why shouldn't I?"

"I didn't say you shouldn't. It's just nice to see you relaxed and happy." Tyler took a sip of coffee. "You *are* happy, right?"

Pembroke leaned back in his chair. They were sitting in Tyler's kitchen, having coffee — or, in Pembroke's case, tea because he disliked coffee — and just being friends. They'd never had the opportunity to do this before. They'd both been in cages when they met, and the circumstances had caused them to become friends, but nothing about their situation had been normal. They'd spent several months in cages next to each other, but after Pembroke had been sold, they hadn't seen each other again until he was rescued.

Pembroke still considered Tyler his best friend. He wouldn't have survived a month without him, and Ryland wouldn't have been able to find him if it weren't for Tyler. Pembroke owed his friend his life, and he didn't think he'd ever be able to repay him.

Not that Tyler wanted to be repaid in any way. Pembroke wouldn't, either, if their roles were reversed.

"I'm getting there," he told his friend.

Tyler's smile turned teasing. "Is it because of a nice lion shifter?"

Pembroke couldn't even hide it, so thankfully he hadn't planned to. Every time he thought of Remington, he found himself daydreaming about what the future held for them. It was a small miracle that Ryland hadn't realized something was happening between them yet, but he would soon if they weren't careful.

Remington didn't want them to be. He wanted to talk to Ryland and be honest, and while Pembroke agreed they should, he was more hesitant.

What if he lost his brother over this?

He'd been without Ryland for a long time. He should have known his brother had never stopped looking for him, but in his darkest moments, he'd wondered. He and Ryland were very different, and Ryland was fifteen years older. They hadn't been that close, even though Ryland had done his best to be a good big brother. Pembroke wouldn't have blamed him if he had stopped looking for him, especially after three years.

But he hadn't. He'd hired Remington and his friend, and even though it had taken three years, they'd found him. That had to mean that Ryland cared about Pembroke, right? He had to want him in his life and wouldn't let anything prevent him from keeping him there, not even a relationship between Pembroke and Remington.

Pembroke didn't know what he'd do if Ryland demanded he choose between him and Remington. Part of him rebelled at that thought. No one could choose who he'd be with except for him, not even his brother. It didn't matter that Ryland had spent hundreds of thousands of dollars and countless hours to find him. He'd done so because he'd felt it was the right thing to do, not because Pembroke had asked for it.

So no, Pembroke didn't want Ryland to choose who he could be with. But on the other hand, he'd just gotten Ryland back after three long years. Could he really choose Remington over his brother?

He was conflicted. If Ryland demanded that Pembroke let go of Remington, he'd be doing the wrong thing. He didn't have the right to choose who Pembroke was with, and that was that. It might mean that Pembroke would lose him, though, and Pembroke didn't think he was ready for that.

"Pem?" Tyler asked.

Pembroke blinked and smiled at him. "Remington is part of the reason I'm happy, yes."

"You haven't told me much about him. Are you together now, or are you still poking at each other to find out if you both want that?"

"We already know we both want it." And even though they hadn't had the talk about being exclusive and dating, they were. "Plus, we're mates."

Pembroke grinned at Tyler's wide eyes. He'd known he'd shock his friend.

"Seriously?" Tyler asked.

"Yeah. We're still working things out, though."

Remington had been clear when they'd talked after Pembroke had twisted his ankle. He wanted him, and if Ryland told him to let go, he wouldn't. Pembroke was that important to him. He was ready to sacrifice his relationship with Ryland because he wanted Pembroke. So it didn't matter if they hadn't talked about being together. They were.

"What have you been up to with him?"

"I don't ask you what you're up to with Matt," Pembroke pointed out.

"And please, never ask. You can't tell me you're doing that with Remington, though. Every time I've seen you together, you kept your distance. That's why I wondered if the two of you were together or not. I know you like him, but I haven't seen you as a couple yet."

"It's complicated," Pembroke said with a sigh. "Remington got to know my brother over the past three years, and I'm the reason they became friends. He says he won't let my brother destroy what's growing between us, and he wants to talk to him, but I'm not sure it's the best idea."

"Do you think Ryland would force the two of you to break up if he knew? Even though you're mates?"

Pembroke took a sip of tea to give himself time to think about that question. "I want to say no, but how can I? I don't really know Ryland anymore, and even before, we weren't that close. I love him, and he's my family, but these past three years have been hard on him. He's overprotective, so I wouldn't be surprised if he wanted to shield me from getting my heart broken. He's also human, so I don't think he fully understands the mate thing."

"He thinks Remington will break your heart?"

"I hope not. Remington says he likes me, and I believe him." No one else would be so patient with Pembroke. Even Pembroke wasn't this patient with himself.

He wanted more than a few kisses and the cuddling he and Remington had shared for now. He wanted to feel desired and cherished, to get back a hint of normal life. He wanted Remington for all of that, but Remington was still adamant that they should talk to Ryland first. He was probably right. Pembroke was focused on his desires and wishes, but Remington knew they'd both regret it if they lost Ryland just because they didn't talk to him.

They didn't have a reason to think that Ryland would tell them to break up. Even though he was overprotective, he had to see that Remington was a perfect guy for Pembroke. He trusted Remington. Wasn't that something he'd want for his brother?

"He's not wrong," Tyler said. "Not talking to your brother would complicate things, and I don't think that's something you want to deal with right now."

"I'm scared he's going to ask me to choose."

"You don't know who you'd choose?"

Pembroke shook his head. How was he supposed to do

that? Ryland was his brother, but Remington felt like he could be Pembroke's future. Pembroke didn't want to give him up, but he didn't want to lose Ryland, either.

He groaned. "Why does everything have to be so complicated?"

Tyler chuckled and patted his shoulder. "It doesn't have to be. There are only a few options here, Pem. Either you immediately break up with Remington and act as if nothing ever happened between the two of you, or you trust Ryland to make the right choice and talk to him before things get too far. If you don't, he'll be hurt that you didn't go to him sooner, which might make him react badly. I think Remington is right. The sooner you do this, the better it will be for everyone."

He was right, but he made it sound so easy. He made *everything* look easy. He hadn't arrived in Rosewood that long ago, yet he already had a boyfriend and a stepdaughter. He'd moved into Matt's house and had made it his home. He was relaxed and happy and looked like he belonged in Rosewood and like he'd always been a pack member. Pembroke, on the other hand, still felt out of place. He hadn't shifted yet because the thought of his hydra form made him want to puke. He didn't hate it, but shifting reminded him of what he'd done for Colbert and of the fights, and he didn't want to think about the people he'd hurt.

Even though he was free, his life was still fucking complicated.

"You're overthinking this," Tyler said. "Ryland doesn't want to lose you, and he'll do whatever he has to so it doesn't happen. If that means not saying anything against you and Remington dating, then I believe that's what he'll do."

"You always have all the answers," Pembroke said.

Tyler laughed. "I don't. I'm still dealing with everything that happened to me, and it's not easy, but you have to remember that you're not alone anymore. You have your brother, me, and the pack. You also have Remington."

Pembroke did, and he was pretty sure that being with Remington would be worth having an uncomfortable conversation with his brother.

He hoped he wouldn't be wrong about that.

Matt eyed Remington. "I'm still not entirely sure why you're here."

Remington had already explained himself to Matt, but he didn't mind doing so a second time. He understood that Matt hadn't been listening to him the first time he'd told him why he was attending the meeting with Matt's lawyer. He was worried about his daughter and focused on her, as he should be.

"I want to talk to your lawyer about your ex-wife and what she's up to."

"That's fine, but he's focusing on Cora's custody. That doesn't have anything to do with what Pamela's doing with Fulton."

"I believe it does."

Matt frowned. "What are you talking about?"

They were meeting at Cam and Toby's house. Pembroke had left to join Tyler, and they were keeping an eye on Matt's daughter. Tyler had wanted to be present during the meeting, but Cora needed some normalcy, and Tyler and Matt felt they couldn't keep handing her over to her friends' mothers or her brothers. Everyone wanted to protect her, and they knew about Pamela and her demands, so they didn't mind, but Matt and Tyler didn't want Cora to be affected by what her mother was doing.

Remington was impressed. Both Tyler and Matt had only Cora's well-being in mind, and while he'd expected that from

Matt, it was a surprise to see that Tyler behaved the same way. The two of them had only recently met, and even though it was clear they loved each other, it couldn't be easy for Tyler to deal with what had happened to him over the past years and become an instant father figure. They were both doing a good job, and the entire pack wanted Cora to be able to stay with them.

Which was where Preston came in. Thankfully, they didn't have to wait long. Preston arrived five minutes early, and Toby showed him to Cam's office. Cam would be sitting in on the meeting, too, which was good because Remington wouldn't have to repeat himself. He might have to explain his thoughts again later, but Cam would be able to tell him if he thought he was right or not.

"Come in," Cam said when Preston stepped into the room. He gestured at the last empty chair in front of his desk, and Preston nodded and went to it.

Remington knew the two of them were friends. That was why Cam had been able to give Preston's name to Matt. Remington sniffed discreetly, curious to find out if Preston was a shifter. He could smell something, but he couldn't identify it. He was pretty sure that Preston was a shifter, but he didn't ask what kind. It would be rude, especially considering how much help Preston was giving them.

Preston sat in the chair and took out a notebook and a pen. Remington was surprised not to see him typing on his phone, but it made him like Preston a little more. He always thought better when he had a pen in his hand, and maybe the same went for Preston.

"I see there's a newcomer today," Preston said. He leaned forward and offered Remington his hand. "Preston Hewitt."

"Remington Barnes."

Preston frowned. "I've heard that name somewhere."

"You might have heard of my company, Barnes & Taylor

Security."

Preston's eyes lit up with understanding. "Is that why you're here today? Are you protecting Matt and his daughter?"

"In a way. I'm not sure how much you've been told about what the pack has been doing."

Preston frowned and turned to Cam. "Please tell me it's nothing illegal."

Cam raised a hand and moved it from side to side. "Some of it is, but we're not going to involve you. You're only here to take care of Matt and his problem with his ex-wife."

"Yet Remington is here, too. What's going on?"

"Remember when I mentioned something about an auction house and people buying and selling shifters?" Cam said.

Remington didn't know how much Cam had told his friend, but it wasn't his place to decide. Cam was the alpha, and his pack was involved. No one would argue with him if he felt that Preston needed to know everything.

Preston groaned. "Don't tell me that Matt's ex-wife is involved."

"She definitely is."

Remington felt almost sorry for Preston. He'd accepted this case when he'd thought it was only a custody battle, but there was much more behind it, and he'd have to deal with that, too.

Or maybe not, depending on what Pamela and Fulton were up to and how the pack and the others wanted to deal with them.

Preston raised a hand. "Okay, let me do this first. I want to update Matt on what's been happening. You can give me all the bad news once I'm done. I can already tell I'm going to need a week to wrap my mind around this mess."

Remington was happy to lean back and let Preston do his thing. They'd have to tell him everything soon enough, anyway.

Cam nodded, and Preston turned his attention to Matt. "I went over the paperwork you sent me, and I was pleased to see that whoever you hired to help you through the adoption process when you first got Cora knew what they were doing. Everything's in order, and your ex-wife won't ever convince a judge to give her custody."

"What about a corrupt judge?" Matt asked.

"That's where things get dicey. She has more than enough money to bribe a judge, and from the research I did into her, I know her fiancé is well-connected. They could create trouble, but the paperwork is solid." He leaned forward. "I don't want you to worry. No matter how many judges they bribe, Cora is *your* daughter. Your ex-wife abandoned her with you and renounced her parental rights. You adopted Cora. The law is clear on all of this. Your ex isn't getting your daughter. It doesn't matter that she gave birth to her.

"Think of it as a normal adoption case. Ignore the fact that Pamela is your ex-wife and focus on the adoption. People adopt children every day through the same process you went through. The mother gives up her rights, and they adopt the child. No one, not even a corrupt judge, will want to upset this balance. I'll still be available if you need me, and I'll keep an eye on your ex's lawyer, but I doubt she'll even manage to get this in front of a judge." Preston leaned back in his chair and looked at Cam. "Now tell me what I don't want to hear."

Cam gestured for Remington to take the lead. That was fine with him.

"Three years ago, I was hired by someone whose brother had vanished. He wanted me to find Pembroke, and I accepted the job and got to work immediately. It took me three years and a lot of help, but eventually, I located Pembroke."

It had taken much more help than Remington wanted to mention here today. He didn't want to overwhelm Preston with names and roles, but he'd email him so that he had every detail he might need.

"During this process, Matt met Tyler, who you already know. We got a deeper insight into the auction house and found out who it belongs to. You mentioned Pamela's fiancé."

"I did," Preston cautiously said as if afraid of what Remington was about to say.

"She's wealthy through him, and *he* is wealthy because he buys and sells rare shifters."

Preston grimaced. "How are you planning on fixing this problem? Will you go to the authorities?"

Cam and Remington exchanged a glance. When Cam didn't say anything, Remington shrugged.

"We could, but will humans care about rare shifters and what happens to them? Besides, with the wealth Fulton has at hand, it would be too easy for him to bribe people, including those judges you were talking about."

"So the pack and your company will take care of them."

"We won't eliminate them if we can avoid it, but yes. This is better taken care of by shifters."

"How does this relate to Pamela wanting her daughter back?"

This was Remington's moment. "I don't think Pamela really wants Cora back. I think she's using her as an excuse to have access to the pack and the rare shifters who live here. She and Fulton deal in rare shifters, and they found an entire group of them here."

Pembroke and Tyler were having fun. Cora was upstairs in Tyler and Matt's bedroom, watching TV there. Tyler was always careful not to allow her downstairs, and Pembroke could see it was taking a toll on his friend. He didn't want Cora to be forbidden in any space of the house, but this was the only way for them to deal with Pamela and Fulton. Hopefully, it wouldn't be long until they could permanently get rid of the two, but in the meantime, Tyler and Matt were doing their best to give Cora the most normal life they could.

Luckily, the little girl didn't seem to realize something was wrong. Pembroke had seen her several times now, and she always appeared happy. She had her father and Tyler, her brothers, and the many friends she'd made when Matt and his family had moved into pack territory. From what little Tyler had shared about their life before Rosewood, Pembroke understood that it was a massive change for all of them, but in a good way.

It was odd to watch Tyler with a child, especially one as old as Cora, but he behaved as if he'd known her for her entire life. She didn't call him Dad, but Pembroke suspected it wouldn't be long until she did. He'd make sure to tease Tyler endlessly when it first happened. Tyler would be delighted anyway.

They'd moved on from talking about Remington and Ryland, but the conversation was interrupted by a knock on the door. Tyler instantly looked alarmed and grabbed his phone from the kitchen table. The kitchen was at the back of the house, so unless whoever was at the door walked around it to spy through the windows, they wouldn't be able to see them.

Tyler unlocked his phone and opened up an app. Pembroke leaned closer to check what his best friend was seeing. He hadn't been surprised when Tyler had explained that he and Matt had bought a smart doorbell. They wanted to be able to see who was there before opening the door.

Tyler swore when Pamela's face appeared on his phone. "Why doesn't she get the hint and leave us alone?" he asked.

"I don't think she can."

Tyler snorted. "There's no way she wants Cora this much.

She abandoned her when she was a baby. She abandoned her three children and didn't return until now. Why can't she live without them anymore? What changed?"

Pembroke hesitated. He didn't want Tyler to freak out more than he already was, but maybe this would help his friend. "She found a massive group of rare shifters."

Tyler frowned. "You've noticed that, too."

"How could I not? Pamela and Fulton deal in rare shifters, and here, they can get many of them. I'm pretty sure Pamela doesn't care about Cora and that she's here just because she wants to take all the rare shifters she can find."

"She's not going to have an easy time with that. Have you met the phoenix twins yet?"

"Only one, I think."

"Lennox?"

Pembroke nodded. He wasn't sure why this was important, but his answer made Tyler smile, so he didn't care.

"Wait until you meet Carey."

Pembroke was curious. He and Tyler had something more important to deal with, though. Distracting Tyler was good, but it wouldn't send Pamela away. "Why don't you call Matt?"

Tyler looked relieved that Pembroke was taking charge. "I should have thought about that right away. He's with Cam and Remington, so one of them will know what to do."

Pembroke ignored the flutter in his stomach at the mention of Remington. He was a lovesick fool, but he needed to focus right now.

Thankfully, Matt answered immediately. He'd probably already found out that Pamela was at the door since he and Tyler had downloaded the app for the doorbell.

"What's she doing?" Pembroke heard Matt ask.

Tyler put the phone call on speaker and placed his phone on the table. "As far as I can see, she's just waiting for me to open."

"Maybe it would be best for you to get out."

"Why? She can't get to us here."

"I don't know. Remington just mentioned something about her and Fulton trying to get to the rare shifters who call Rosewood their home, and I'm afraid he's right."

"That's what Pembroke said, too."

"You two are both rare shifters. You shouldn't stay in the house when there's a chance that she might get you."

"How could she ever think to take us both at the same time?" Pembroke asked.

"She might have a way to make you unconscious. I don't know, Pem. I just know that we'd all feel better if you, Tyler, and Cora left the house. We're on our way, but I want you as far away from her as possible."

Pembroke wasn't sure it was a good idea, but he wasn't the idea guy here. If Matt was asking them to leave the house, then they should. Besides, if Pamela confronted them, it would be better if they were in the open. Here, Pembroke couldn't shift without breaking half the house down.

Tyler was pale but moved swiftly as he rushed out of the kitchen to get Cora. Pembroke stayed where he was, staring down at the phone still on the table. Pamela was still knocking, and worse, she was trying to open the door. Tyler had locked it, but it might not be enough to stop her from coming in.

Thankfully, it didn't take Tyler long to be back with Cora. She looked confused, while Tyler was terrified, so Pembroke decided to take the situation in hand. "Hey," he told Cora as he crouched in front of her. "I thought we could play hide and seek in the forest."

Her smile lit up the room. "Really?"

"Yeah. You and Tyler are going to run in the forest, and I'll stay back and start counting, all right?"

"You need to come with us," Tyler interjected.

Pembroke got to his feet. "I'll stay and make sure she can't get to you," he murmured. "Your main focus needs to be Cora and to keep her safe. I'll be fine. From what I can see, there's no one here but Pamela, and if she tries anything, I can just shift and stomp on her. Besides, Matt and the others are almost here. Don't worry about me, focus on your daughter."

It was clear from Tyler's expression that he wanted to argue, but Pembroke pushed him toward the door. Cora was pulling him, eager to start their game, and Tyler eventually gave in.

"We need to be quiet because otherwise, Uncle Pem will find us," he told the little girl.

She seemed to take this seriously, which was a relief. The two of them rushed out the door, Pembroke right behind them. For a moment, he thought they'd make it out without encountering Pamela. Tyler and Cora reached the forest just a few seconds after leaving the house, and Pembroke was behind them.

Pembroke heard hurried footsteps behind him. He wasn't in the forest but at the edge of it. He could vanish between the trees and hope Pamela wouldn't find them, but how could he do that? He needed to protect Tyler and Cora, even if that meant facing Pamela.

There was nothing he wanted less. Pamela belonged to his past, and he wanted to forget about all of it. Just thinking about her reminded him of things he never wanted to think about again.

But Tyler and Cora were worth it. They were worth Pembroke defending them and shifting into his hydra form.

He quickly took off his shoes and his jeans. That was all he had the time to take off before Pamela appeared. She grinned when she saw him, but her eyes widened as she took in the fact that he was standing there in his sweater and boxer briefs.

Pembroke shifted.

Remington was in good shape, but it might not be enough to make it out of the forest alive. He kept stumbling on roots and almost falling on his face, and the timing was inconvenient, to say the least.

Pamela was at Matt and Tyler's house, trying to get to them.

Remington hated that she was even able to get into pack territory, but he agreed with Cam that it was the best way for them to keep an eye on her and what she was doing. If they behaved as if they believed that she just wanted Cora back, then maybe she'd make mistakes and expose herself and Fulton.

Remington didn't think that mattered anymore. She had to know they weren't stupid and that they suspected she had another goal. Even if she didn't, it would be understandable if Cam ordered her out. Matt was a pack member, and Cam's job was to protect him and Cora against anything that might hurt them.

That included Pamela.

The sound of someone running toward them made Remington tense. He glanced sideways at Cam and Matt, who were running with him in the forest. Cam noticed and nodded, which meant he and Remington were both ready to intervene, whatever was about to happen. Remington figured Matt was distracted by the thought of what might be happening to Cora and Tyler, so he didn't expect him to be of any help during the fight.

But they didn't have to fight. Two figures crashed between the trees, and Matt cried out at the sight of Tyler and Cora. Cora was happy to see her father and threw herself at him, and Matt caught her easily, hauling her into his arms. As soon as he was sure she was safe, he grabbed Tyler and pulled him close.

"Where's Pembroke?" Remington asked.

Tyler's eyes went wide as he answered. "He stayed back. He said he would make sure that Pamela couldn't get to us. I tried to get him to change his mind, but he wouldn't listen."

That sounded exactly like Pembroke, so Remington wasn't surprised. He still wished he could give his boyfriend a good shake and ask him what the fuck he was thinking.

*Later.* Right now, he needed to get to him. He didn't think Pamela would try anything, but he didn't trust her.

He continued running while Cam took a moment to make sure Tyler and Cora were all right. Remington could take care of one human woman. He could shift into his lion form and eat her, if it came to that.

But he didn't have to. When he reached the edge of the forest behind Matt and Tyler's house, he saw Pembroke in his hydra form, facing away from Remington. He was standing strong, facing someone. There was no doubt in Remington's mind that Pamela was on the other side of Pembroke, and since Pembroke seemed to be all right, he took a moment to breathe.

He'd seen Pembroke's hydra form before but hadn't had the opportunity to really look at it. That day had been a mess of people running around screaming, and they'd needed to get Pembroke out as soon as possible.

Pembroke was massive in this form, almost the same size as the house he stood close to. He had three heads, each of them atop a long snake-like neck. His body was scaly and a dark blue and gray mix. The heads dropped down to face someone. Remington was almost afraid Pembroke would eat Pamela, so he rushed around him.

He shouldn't have worried. The only thing he saw of Pamela was her back as she ran away from Pembroke, screaming as if he were killing her. She was wearing high heels and fell on her knees before reaching the house. That wasn't enough to stop her. She scrambled to her feet and continued running, leaving Pembroke and Remington behind.

Remington waited until she'd disappeared and he heard the sound of her car driving away before turning to Pembroke.

He was still in his hydra form. Remington knew he'd been hesitant to shift back after spending so much time in that form. It was good to see that he hadn't hesitated today, although Remington wished he hadn't needed to do it to protect someone. It wasn't fair to ask this of him.

"Everything all right?" he asked.

All three of Pembroke's heads lowered toward him.

He swallowed—even knowing that Pembroke would never hurt him, he was still impressive in this form, and he could hurt Remington pretty badly if he tried.

He didn't. Instead, his middle head bumped against Remington's chest. Remington realized what Pembroke wanted and laughed, relieved to see that his boyfriend was all right and demanding to be petted.

He obliged. Pembroke's skin was soft and, to Remington's surprise, warm. He wasn't sure why, but he'd expected Pembroke to be cold-blooded.

He scratched Pembroke on top of the head. "You did a good job," he said with a smile. "I don't think I've ever seen anyone running so quickly."

Pembroke huffed. He probably didn't need to be praised for something like this, but Remington wanted him to know that everyone appreciated what he'd done.

He'd stayed behind to protect his friend. Many people wouldn't have done that. They would have run even faster than Tyler and left him behind,

Remington was startled when Pembroke shifted back.

Pembroke's sweater was toast, as was his underwear, but he'd thought of taking his shoes and jeans off before shifting, so they were safe. Remington quickly took off his own sweater, and as soon as Pembroke was close enough, he wrapped it around his shoulders.

Pembroke gave him a grateful smile and took it off to slide it on. "Thank you. I would have been cold without this."

Remington felt cold with only a t-shirt, but he wasn't planning to stay there long. He just wanted Pembroke to be warm, and he was ready to sacrifice his comfort to ensure he was.

"You stood up to one of your jailers," he said.

Pembroke shrugged. "It was easy. She wasn't surrounded by guards here, so she freaked out as soon as I shifted."

"Still. I'm proud of you." Remington kissed the top of Pembroke's head. He was relieved when Pembroke leaned against him. He knew this had been hard for Pembroke, and not just because he'd had to face Pamela. He'd shifted into his hydra form for the first time since he'd been rescued, even though he'd been avoiding it.

"I still don't understand why she's allowed in pack territory so easily," Pembroke complained.

"Cam thought it would be the best way to catch her in the act of whatever she and Fulton are planning."

"Kidnapping a bunch of rare shifters who live with the Rosewood pack?"

So Remington wasn't the only one thinking that was what they were planning. "I suppose. I feel we need to talk about it, though. It's becoming too dangerous to allow her to walk in and out as much as she wants. Besides, she has to know we don't believe she's here for Cora."

"Maybe she'll stay away."

Remington could only hope Pembroke was right, but what would be the odds?

He didn't know Pamela and Fulton as well as Tyler and

Pembroke did, but he could already tell this wouldn't be enough to stop them. They were greedy, and they wanted more rare shifters to sell. The only way they'd obtain that was by kidnapping them, and here in Rosewood, they'd find plenty of them. The shifters would defend themselves and might even win some of the fights, but Pamela and Fulton could hire countless guards to help them. If they did, the pack would be in trouble, and they couldn't afford for that to happen.

They needed to get rid of the evil couple, and they had to do it sooner rather than later.

# CHAPTER SIX

Pembroke was ready for more. He loved what he and Remington had, but he felt the need to scream every time Remington snatched his hand away from him or stepped back when someone saw them together. He was ready to come out to the world and his brother about what was happening between him and Remington and them being mates, and he prayed Remington felt the same.

They'd been getting to know each other, and it had been great. Pembroke didn't sleep a lot because of the nightmares, and Remington had taken to going on walks with him every time he woke up and couldn't get back to sleep. It meant Remington had to wake up, but he'd promised Pembroke that he didn't mind, and Pembroke loved that he wasn't alone during the night anymore.

But even without Remington, he wouldn't have been. That was a big change, too. *Pembroke wasn't alone anymore.* He wasn't isolated in a cage, kept away from everyone. Any time he needed to talk, he could call Tyler, Peregrine, or any of the people who wanted to be his friend.

It felt like half the pack had visited him to let him know that if he needed anything, he just had to reach out. The rare shifters especially had made a point of telling him they felt part of the same family. Pembroke had lived with rare shifters before, but the situation had been very different. They'd all been forced to be there and hadn't wanted to make friends. Pembroke had felt the same. Here, though, everyone was friendly, and while it was overwhelming, it made him feel like he *was* part of a family.

He wanted to stay in Rosewood. Ryland had already suggested they could both do so, and Pembroke was pretty sure that Remington would, too. He'd caught him talking with Toby and Leslie, one of the pack's betas. He hadn't thought anything of it, but Remington had been mysterious about that conversation for some reason. Pembroke didn't like that they had secrets, even though he was pretty sure it wasn't anything bad. At the moment, he disliked secrets entirely and had had enough of them.

He went to look for Remington in the kitchen, where he could usually be found in the morning. The room was empty except for a sleepy Toby, who was setting up the coffee machine and appeared relieved when Pembroke waved at him but didn't stick around.

The next obvious stop was Remington's bedroom. The guest rooms were in the same hallway, meaning that Pembroke, Remington, and Ryland had their rooms there. It made things awkward with Remington because they needed to be careful not to be caught when they spent time together, especially early in the morning after one of Pembroke's nightmares.

He knocked, and when Remington called out to come in, he pushed open the door. He scurried inside and closed it again, leaning against it as he looked toward the bathroom door. It was open, and Pembroke could see a bare-chested Remington shaving from where he was.

Pembroke swallowed. He couldn't believe this man was his. Sometimes it didn't feel like he was, but that was Pembroke's fault.

He didn't blame Remington for wanting to talk to Ryland before things went any further between them. It made him want to bitch because he wasn't a child, and Remington didn't need to ask for Ryland's permission to date him, but that wasn't why Remington wanted to talk to Ryland. He wanted to be honest with him before Ryland realized something was happening and thought they'd hidden it from him.

They had.

Remington smiled at Pembroke. "I didn't expect you to visit so early. How did you sleep?"

Pembroke's heart felt like it was about to explode. Remington always checked in and cared for him, and he loved that. "I'm ready," he blurted out.

Remington blinked. Half of his face was still covered in shaving cream, but it didn't take away from his sexiness. This peek into a familiar routine made Pembroke want to see it every day.

"What are you ready for?" Remington asked. His movements were sure and precise, but it was clear he was ready to be done.

"I want us to take the next step in our relationship, and we can only do that if we talk to Ryland. That's what I'm ready to do. I want to talk to him and tell him you and I are mates."

"Are you sure?"

Pembroke wasn't surprised that Remington was asking that. He didn't want Pembroke to regret being with him, something that might happen if Ryland decided he wanted nothing to do with any of this. Pembroke prayed his brother wouldn't be such an asshole. "I am. I've been thinking about it, and while I know I need time to heal and get over what happened to me, I don't want to wait that long for you and me to be together. I feel that what we have is good for me, and I'm done hiding. I want more. I want to be able to take your hand and kiss you without having to think twice about it and wonder if anyone will see us."

"What if Ryland doesn't take this well?"

Pembroke sighed. "I'll be honest. I don't want to think about that possibility."

"It's something you should think about before you make any decision." Remington put down his razor and quickly rinsed his face.

"I know. I don't want to lose Ryland, but I don't like the outcome when I think of choosing him over you. No matter how much I want him in my life, if he forces me to choose between the two of you, I'll come to resent him. I'll be angry, and by the end of it, I'll have lost both of you. I don't think he'll ask me to choose, but if he does, I'll choose you." Pembroke sucked in a breath. "I'm in love with you."

Remington strode out of the bathroom. His skin was still damp, but Pembroke didn't care because Remington kissed him.

"I'm in love with you, too," Remington murmured. "I'm glad you're finally ready to do this."

Pembroke wrapped his arms around Remington's waist. "It's going to hurt both of us if he asks us to choose, but we'll get through it together."

Remington nodded. "We will." He hesitated, then kissed the top of Pembroke's head. "There's something I want to tell you."

Pembroke looked up and grinned. "Are you ready to tell me what you've been plotting behind my back?"

Remington laughed. "Not plotting behind your back. I just wanted to be sure everything was ready before I told you about it. I didn't want to push you into making a decision before you were ready."

"Well, I'm ready to hear whatever you have to say."

Remington didn't let go of Pembroke, which Pembroke loved. His hold was loose enough that Pembroke could step away if he wanted to, but why would he? He felt so good in Remington's arms. They cradled him, made him feel cherished and protected at the same time, and like he belonged.

"I've been talking to Cam and Toby. I didn't tell them

about us. Although, I'm pretty sure that at least Toby suspects we're together, but I told them that I want to move here. They were happy because it means the rare shifters and the pack will have more protection."

"Is that the only reason they were happy?"

Remington shrugged one shoulder. "I'm pretty sure they like me, too, but considering the situation and what we know is coming, it's good that the pack will have more protection. I can help, of course, but not just me. Braden and I have been talking about opening a second office, and while Rosewood might be a little small to do so, there are plenty of big cities around here. It's not like I have to be in the office every day once it's established. It's going to take a while, and I'll have to work a lot, but once everything is done, I can work from here."

"So you're moving to Rosewood."

"I am. Cam talked to me a few days ago and gave me a choice between a few houses. All of them are solid, but they need renovations, especially if I'm going to spend the rest of my life there. I chose one. I've already been there and cleaned up, and thankfully, the pack was able to lend me the furniture I need until I buy my own, but it's done. I have a house in Rosewood."

Pembroke's heart raced. He knew what Remington wasn't saying. It was way too soon for them to move in together, but eventually, that house would become Pembroke's home, too. The thought scared Pembroke as much as it excited him. It was everything he'd thought he'd lost after he'd been kidnapped and so much more.

But until he knew how things went with Ryland, Pembroke felt he couldn't really enjoy any of it. He couldn't make promises to Remington, no matter how much he wanted to.

"You'll show me your house later today, all right? First, I want to talk to Ryland."

Unfortunately, Ryland was already gone by the time they left Remington's bedroom. He'd left a note to Pembroke telling him that he had several meetings and that he'd be back that night. Remington wasn't surprised, but he could tell Pembroke wished they'd done this sooner. Now that he'd made his decision, he wanted to take the next step, and they couldn't do so without talking to Ryland.

Remington decided to take things in hand. If he left it to Pembroke, he'd probably call his brother and blurt everything out over the phone. That wouldn't be the best way to do it and would no doubt lead to Ryland freaking out and maybe yelling, which was something they were trying to avoid. Doing anything on the phone was out, but that was a good thing. Remington knew Ryland like the back of his hand. They'd been friends for the past three years, and they'd seen each other every day. Pembroke had brought them together, and Remington prayed he wouldn't pull them apart.

He wanted to make this as easy as possible on everyone, which meant getting Ryland alone and in a place where no one would care if he freaked out. They didn't have much privacy in the house because Cam and Toby were always around, so that was the first thing Remington decided to take care of.

He knocked on Cam's office door, waited for the alpha to go out for him to enter, and did so.

"I have a favor to ask," he opened with.

Cam looked surprised. "I'm listening."

Remington was uncomfortable telling Cam about him and Pembroke before they told Ryland, but Cam was the pack alpha. By moving into pack territory, Remington had become a pack member. They hadn't made it official, but they didn't need to. It was implied, and that meant that Cam was now his alpha.

"Pembroke and I have to talk to Ryland today. We need a quiet place where he won't care if he has a breakdown."

Cam grinned and leaned back in his chair. "Are you ready to tell him the two of you are dating?"

Remington groaned. "You know?"

"Toby and I suspected. Well, Toby did. I swear that he has eyes in the back of his head. I didn't see anything until he mentioned it, and once he did, it was kind of obvious. I'm not surprised Ryland doesn't know about it yet, though."

"We want to rectify that today. Pembroke is ready to talk to his brother and tell him we're mates, but I need to carefully plan how and where we do this."

"I can take Toby out on a date," Cam offered. "It's been a while, and considering what's coming, I wouldn't mind taking advantage of our relative peace and spending time with him. That would give you, Pembroke, and Ryland the house for the evening. Maybe you can cook dinner and talk to Ryland over food. Food always makes things better."

Remington couldn't stop himself from smiling. "Does it?"

"Especially if it's Toby's lasagna. How about I ask him to make it for the three of you?"

"Oh, it's not necessary. I'm sure we can find something to eat without him having to slave away in the kitchen."

"He enjoys cooking. Besides, he'll be happy when he finds out you and Pembroke are mates, and he'll want to celebrate in his own way."

It was good to know that even if Ryland didn't take the news well, Pembroke and Remington weren't alone. Cam and Toby clearly supported their relationship, which was huge, considering that Cam was the alpha. It wouldn't help change Ryland's mind if he decided to be a stubborn asshole, but it helped to know Remington and Pembroke had support.

Once Remington knew dinner at home was a go, he texted

Ryland to let him know about it, then went to find Pembroke. He doubted he'd be able to focus on his job today, so he also texted Braden to warn him. Remington was in the process of moving, and Braden had teased him that he'd be useless for the next few weeks so he wouldn't be surprised. Remington had promised that wouldn't happen, but at least today, he needed the day off.

But there was still a lot of time until dinner, and Remington could feel his skin crawling with anticipation. He needed to do something to distract himself, and what better than to focus on his home?

After Remington talked to Pembroke, Pembroke left to go into town with Tyler and Peregrine. Remington had more than enough work to do. His house was nice enough, but he didn't want it just to be a house. He wanted this place to be a home, and to do so, he had to work on it.

It would be fairly easy. He knew a lot of people through his job, and between that and Toby's help, he managed to find someone who would do the renovations. It was a pack member, which made everything easier. Once they'd agreed on a meeting, Remington cleaned up a little more in case Pembroke wanted to visit. The house wasn't what it would be yet, but it could still be clean and comfortable.

He was still working when a knock on the door startled him. He looked out the window next to the front door, surprised to see it was already dark. Of course, it didn't take much since it was January.

He quickly washed and dried his hands, then went to open. Ryland stood there, and he glanced behind Remington right away as if he expected to find someone. For a moment, Remington worried that Ryland had found out he and Pembroke were together. It got worse when Ryland opened his mouth.

"Is Pembroke here?"

Remington swallowed and gestured at his friend to come in. "No. Should he be?"

"He's not at the house."

"He's probably still in town with his friends."

Ryland's eyes widened. "In town?"

Remington knew where this was going. He understood why Ryland was worried, but since Pembroke wasn't here to stand up for himself, Remington would do it for him. "He's perfectly safe. Half the town is made up of pack members, and he's with Tyler and Peregrine."

"Peregrine is a pigeon shifter. He can't protect Pembroke."

"Maybe not, but Tyler can, and Pembroke can protect himself."

Ryland was still tense. Remington waited for him to explode and start calling Pembroke to get him to come home, but it didn't happen.

Ryland's shoulders relaxed. It was obvious he was doing it mindfully and that it wasn't easy, but he did it and smiled at Remington. "You're right. I need to stop freaking out every time my brother does something like this."

"You're scared something will happen to him, and it's understandable. But you can't force him to stay in pack territory or, worse, in Cam's house. That would be exchanging one cell for another, and I don't think you want to do that to your brother."

Ryland shook his head and leaned against the wall. They could be more comfortable by going to the kitchen or the living room, but it seemed that Ryland was fine speaking here.

"I know I've been a lot lately. I'm surprised he's going along with it as much as he has been, to be honest."

"He knows why you feel like this, and I think that after three years, he wants to give you what you need."

Ryland nodded. "I get it, but I want to give him what he needs, too. I don't like that it's more freedom, but he's twenty-five. He's an adult, and with everything he's been through, he had to grow up a lot faster than most twenty-five-year-olds. I can't continue to do this if I don't want him to kick me out of his life. It's hard to resist the instinct to freak out whenever I can't see him."

Remington felt for his friend. He wanted to reassure Ryland that everything would be okay, but he couldn't because there was no way for him to know that. Both of them could only hope that whatever happened next, Pembroke would be safe.

"Come on. Help me finish what I was doing. Then we can head back to Cam's house and have dinner. I'm sure Pembroke will be there by the time we arrive."

Thankfully, that was enough to distract Ryland. Remington couldn't help but wonder if he could be distracted from freaking out after he and Pembroke told him they were together.

Pembroke had spent the day with his friends, and he'd loved it. He'd been apprehensive initially, jumping at every strange noise and expecting someone to grab him from behind every time they walked past a van, but he'd quickly gotten over it. Being able to spend time with Tyler out of the cage was incredible, and Peregrine's presence made it even better.

The three of them had become fast friends. Pembroke and Tyler were closer than ever, and Peregrine fit seamlessly with them. Pembroke already couldn't imagine his life here without them, and he couldn't even think about leaving Rosewood. No matter what Ryland wanted or decided, this was Pembroke's home now, and he wouldn't let anyone take it away from him, not even his brother.

Especially not him.

Pembroke was afraid of Ryland's reaction when he found

out Pembroke and Remington were mates, but he wouldn't give in. He could understand why Ryland was trying to protect him, but there was nothing to protect him from when it came to Remington. He was one of the nicest people Pembroke had ever met, and he trusted him as much as he trusted Tyler or Ryland.

"You worry too much," Tyler said from the passenger seat of Peregrine's car.

Being in a car with Peregrine at the wheel had been an experience. He'd gotten his license only a few weeks ago, and he was both apprehensive and glad to have more freedom. He wasn't a bad driver, but he alternated between being too cautious and telling anyone else on the road to fuck off. He was hilarious, but Pembroke had feared for his life a few times.

"You'd worry, too, if your brother was about to tell you to choose between him and your mate," Pembroke grumbled.

Tyler twisted in his seat to look at Pembroke. "He's not going to tell you to choose between them."

"You can't know that."

"I think I can. Ryland is your brother, but you haven't seen him for three years. You've been spending a lot of time with him now, but you still see the man he was three years ago instead of the man he is now. I got to know him, Pem. He'll do anything if it means keeping you in his life, including being happy for you and Remington."

"He's overprotective."

"As would anyone be, considering what happened to you. You can't blame him for being worried."

"I don't." He really didn't. He was just worried about what Ryland would say when he found out about this.

It wouldn't be long now. Peregrine was driving them back to pack territory, and Pembroke and Remington were having dinner with Ryland. Remington had texted that Cam and Toby had left for date night, so the house would be empty except for the three of them. Ryland could yell at them as loudly as he wanted, but Pembroke hoped he wouldn't.

He didn't want to make his brother angry. Ryland had been through a lot over the past three years, and while he *was* overprotective, he was only that way because he wanted Pembroke to be safe. Pembroke had been through hell, but when he thought about being in Ryland's place, he couldn't even imagine how hard it had been to wonder if Pembroke was dead or alive and what was happening to him for three long years.

"Everything will be fine," Peregrine promised as he turned onto the small road that led to the heart of pack territory where Cam and Toby's house was.

Both he and Tyler lived deeper in the forest, but most pack members left their cars there. It was easier to do that and walk the rest of the way than to try to open a road in the middle of the woods.

"I hope you're right," Pembroke murmured.

When Peregrine parked the car, Pembroke knew the time was up. The three of them said their goodbyes, and he watched Peregrine and Tyler walk away. Part of him wanted to go with them, but another wanted this to end. Once it did, Pembroke could stop hiding that he loved Remington, and he was so fucking ready for that.

He climbed the porch steps two by two and threw open the door. Remington had texted that Toby was cooking, and Pembroke's stomach growled as soon as he stepped into the house and the smell of dinner hit him. It smelled like garlic and tomato sauce, and Pembroke tried to remember the last time he'd had lasagna. Probably before he'd been kidnapped.

"We're in the kitchen," Ryland called out.

Pembroke took off his jacket and shoes, took a deep breath, and went to join them.

The lasagna was still in the oven, and Remington and

Ryland were seated at the table. They'd been talking, but Ryland got to his feet as soon as Pembroke entered the room. Pembroke expected his brother to berate him for going into town without letting him know, but instead, Ryland pulled him into his arms. He kissed the top of Pembroke's head, and Pembroke relaxed and hoped this wasn't the last hug they'd share.

"I'm sorry if I've been overprotective since I got you back," Ryland said. "I only did it because I worry about you."

"I know, and I'm not angry."

Ryland stepped back and nodded. "That's good, and I promise I'll try to take a step back. No matter what happened to you, you're an adult, and Rosewood is safe."

The three of them knew that might not be true with Pamela and Fulton breathing down their necks, but Pembroke refused to hide. He'd been locked up for three years. His second chance wouldn't be another cell.

"Let's eat," Remington said as he got up and went to open the oven.

Pembroke wanted to hug him, but instead, he washed his hands and sat at the table with Ryland. It was already set, so as soon as Remington dished out the meal, they started eating.

Pembroke had been so nervous that he'd barely eaten today, and now, he stuffed himself with pasta and garlic goodness. He made sure not to eat too much in case this conversation didn't go well. He didn't think he'd throw up even if Ryland told him that he needed to break up with Remington, but he wouldn't know for sure unless it happened.

"I'm glad we did this," Ryland said once he was done eating and leaning back in his chair. Had he eaten too much? He kept rubbing his stomach as if he were pregnant.

Remington and Pembroke looked at each other. Was now the right time? Should they wait until they digested the meal? Pembroke bit his lower lip. He'd come to realize there would never be a perfect moment to be honest with his brother. He and Remington just needed to say it.

He sucked in a breath. "I'm glad we had dinner together, too. I like spending time with you. Since everyone is here, I wanted to tell you that Remington and I are mates."

The silence that followed Pembroke's declaration was heavy. Pembroke had to resist the urge to screw his eyes shut and stick his fingers into his ears so he wouldn't hear what his brother had to say. He was afraid to look up, but Remington wasn't. He faced Ryland head-on and reached over the table to grab one of Pembroke's hands. Pembroke felt better once their fingers tangled together, and he was finally brave enough to look at his brother.

Ryland was gaping at them. For now, surprise was the only reaction he seemed to be having.

He opened his mouth to say something, but the only thing that came out was a croak. He cleared his throat and tried again, and Pembroke steeled himself for what was coming.

"When did this happen?" Ryland asked.

"We realized we were mates a few days after Pembroke arrived. I've been spending some time with him because he has nightmares, and we've gotten to know each other," Remington said. "We decided we needed to talk to you before things became too serious, but the fact that we're mates means that things were always serious. I want to make Pembroke happy for the rest of my life."

Ryland swallowed heavily. "You're in love with him?"

Remington nodded. He wasn't ashamed of being honest.

Pembroke loved that. "I'm in love with him, too," he said as he got to his feet. He had so much nervous energy that he needed to burn. He started pacing the kitchen. "So please, don't ask me to choose between the two of you. I don't think I can." He frowned. "Actually, I can. If you ask me to choose, I'll choose my mate because I love him."

To Pembroke's surprise, Ryland laughed. He got up, too, and came to stand in front of Pembroke. "Why would I ask you to choose? I'm not going to decide who you can fall in love with, especially when it comes to your mate. Besides, I know Remington. I trust and respect him, and there isn't a better man out there for you."

Pembroke wasn't going to cry, dammit. This was a happy moment, and it didn't call for tears.

They still spilled out of his eyes as he hugged his brother. When he was done, he turned, and of course Remington was there, too. Pembroke threw himself into his arms, happy to finally be able to do it without having to hide.

"We can talk tomorrow," Ryland said. "Pembroke looks like he needs a moment to wrap his mind around what happened, so why don't the two of you go?"

Pembroke looked up at Remington. "Can we?"

"Of course. We can do whatever you want," Remington said.

"Then take me home, please. Take me to your house."


Remington couldn't say he hadn't expected this. Pembroke had been honest when he'd told him what he wanted, and he'd never hidden the fact that it was for them to be together. Now that Ryland knew what was happening and was okay with it, it made sense that Pembroke was ready for more.

He'd been ready for a while now, and so had Remington. They'd just needed to talk to Ryland, and now that they had, nothing was keeping them apart.

"I'd be over the moon if you wanted to come with me," Remington said. "The house is furnished, but it's a bit of a mess. I hope that's not a problem."

Pembroke rolled his eyes. Every time Remington spent time with him, he saw more and more of him. Pembroke had been afraid, and for three years, people had pushed him down every time he tried to surface. Here in Rosewood, he was safe, and he could be himself.

"Why would it be a problem? I spent three years in a cage. Do you really think I'll be angry because you don't have a couch?"

"I do have a couch." And a bed, but Remington wasn't sure that was what Pembroke wanted yet. "I just wanted you to know what you were about to find."

Pembroke stepped closer and hooked his arms around Remington's neck. "I doubt I'll be looking at anything but you, anyway."

The same went for Remington. Now that he had Pembroke, he couldn't imagine not making him the center of his life. The way Pembroke looked at him made him want to cherish him, and he couldn't wait to give his boyfriend anything he could ask for.

Remington couldn't remember the last time he'd felt so strongly for anyone. He'd had relationships, and some of them had lasted for years. He'd loved the people he'd been with, but Pembroke was special. He was resilient, strong, and incredibly sweet, even after what had happened to him. He wouldn't hesitate to fight for what he wanted, but at the same time, he was willing to let Remington take care of him and keep him safe. He needed Remington, but he also didn't, and Remington loved both those things.

"Let's go home," Pembroke murmured.

*Home.* Remington was making himself a home in Rosewood, surrounded by the pack, and it felt almost too good to be true. His life was changing, but he didn't mind. If anything, he enjoyed what it was becoming and couldn't wait to see what happened next.

He stepped away from Pembroke, took his hand, and pulled him out of the room. He heard Ryland laugh behind them, and his heart soared. His best friend hadn't told them that he was fine with them being together just because he thought it was what they wanted to hear. He'd told them that because he really was okay with it, and it meant a lot to Remington to know that. He wouldn't have stopped even if Ryland hadn't been okay with this, but he wanted Pembroke to have everything he could dream of, and that included Ryland. Pembroke wouldn't have truly been happy if his brother hadn't been in his life.

That wasn't something they needed to worry about. Ryland was fine with them being together, and he wouldn't try to stop them or take Pembroke away. They were all moving to Rosewood, where they could start a new life.

Pembroke laughed, too, as Remington dragged him out of the house. They'd stopped to put on shoes and jackets, and once they were outside in the falling snow, Remington slowed down. He wanted to take Pembroke home, but they deserved to enjoy this moment.

"It's beautiful," Pembroke breathed out.

Remington looked at him. "You're beautiful."

Pembroke huffed. "You know what I mean."

"I do, and I said the truth. You *are* beautiful, and I'm so glad you chose me."

Pembroke looked at Remington. His cheeks were red, his lips parted, and he'd never been so beautiful. Remington could hardly believe this young, vibrant man wanted him, but he wasn't going to deny him this. He'd been lucky and had every intention of clinging on as hard as he could for as long as Pembroke allowed him to.

They didn't rush home, but they also didn't turn this into a slow walk. They were both impatient, and while Remington wished the house was ready for Pembroke, Pembroke wouldn't care. He just wanted to be with Remington, just like Remington wanted to be with him. It didn't matter where that happened, but Remington was glad it would be out of Cam's house. Ryland was still staying there, and it would have been awkward, to say the least.

But Remington had his own house now, and it was good that he hadn't managed to do more than clean it up. He wanted Pembroke to feel like the house was his, too, even though that was rushing into things. He didn't expect Pembroke to move in with him right away, but he hoped that eventually it would happen, and when it did, Pembroke needed to feel like he belonged there. That was why Remington was planning on asking for his input on the renovations and the new furniture.

But it wasn't something he needed to worry about tonight. Tonight, both he and Pembroke had better things to focus on.

They barely paused to take off their jackets when they reached the house. It was pleasantly warm, a stark contrast with the cold outside. It made Pembroke's cheeks flush deeper, and Remington had a hard time resisting him. Then, he realized he didn't have to resist him because Pembroke wanted him. He wanted them to be together, which was why he was here.

Remington pulled Pembroke into his arms and kissed him. Pembroke was still hopping as he took off one of his shoes, but he sank against Remington's body, sighing in pleasure as his body relaxed. He felt perfect in Remington's arms, and Remington couldn't believe he'd managed to resist this for so long. It had been the right thing to do, and he was glad it was over.

"Where's your bedroom?" Pembroke asked, looking up the stairs.

"Don't you want something to drink first? Or maybe to talk?"

Pembroke glared. "Don't you try to slow us down. I've been wanting to get my hands on you since I first saw you, even though I was confused and scared. Everything is out of the way now, so you can't deny me."

Remington chuckled. He felt lighter than he had in a long time. "I'm not planning to."

Pembroke grinned. "Good." He grabbed Remington's hand and hauled him toward the stairs. He climbed them two by two, and Remington had to hurry to keep up with him. Once they were upstairs, he took the lead since Pembroke didn't know where the bedroom was yet.

This was the one place where Remington had made sure everything was as it should be. He was planning on renovating the bathroom, but the bedroom was nice enough, and with a new mattress and new sheets, the bed was comfortable. It was big enough for him, Pembroke, and a few other people, but he wasn't planning to invite anyone but Pembroke there. He liked his space when he slept and hoped Pembroke wouldn't mind.

He didn't ask because, at the moment, Pembroke was focused on one thing and one thing only.

Getting Remington naked and in bed.

He pushed Remington to the mattress, and as soon as Remington landed, he dove for Remington's jeans. Remington laughed again and tried to remember the last time sex had been this fun. It was always intense, good most of the time, but not as lighthearted and loving.

And he'd get to have this for the rest of his life.

It was incredible, but he wouldn't have it any other way. His relationship with Pembroke would last for a long time, which was what he wanted and needed.

Pembroke made a triumphant sound and pulled Remington's jeans down his legs. Remington helped by raising his hips, and as soon as the jeans were off his legs, he took off his sweater. Pembroke's hands were on his stomach and his sides as he explored his body before he was even fully naked.

Remington wanted more, but not like this.

"I'm not having sex with my socks on," he said as soon as his head was free from his t-shirt.

Pembroke cackled. "That's where you draw the line?"

"Pretty much. There's nothing worse than sex with socks on, and I don't care how cold it is." He looked Pembroke up and down. "And you're not naked enough for this."

Pembroke grinned. "I'll take care of it."

He did so quickly. Remington wanted to look at his body and enjoy it, but they'd been waiting for this moment for a while. They were both excited and impatient, so it wasn't a surprise when, as soon as he was naked, Pembroke dove onto the mattress. He bounced next to Remington, who was already rolling to his side and pulling him on top of him.

Pembroke's knees bracketed Remington's hips. They were both hard, and their cocks bumped together as Pembroke leaned forward to kiss Remington. Remington groaned and slid his hands from Pembroke's hips to his ass, gripping it as he hauled Pembroke closer.

He wanted more. He wanted Pembroke in him and to be in Pembroke. He wanted them to be one.

But this was good, too. They were both impatient and aiming for only one thing.

They'd have time to explore and go slow later, and that knowledge made Remington feel better. This wouldn't be a one-time thing he had to enjoy as much as possible. He and Pembroke would have this for the rest of their lives.

He suspected that was the main reason Pembroke didn't push for more. He knew this was only the first step in their physical relationship, so he was happy grinding against Remington and rubbing their cocks together as they moved.

Remington held him down as he raised his hips. Thankfully, Pembroke leaned down to kiss Remington, which pressed their cocks between their stomachs and added friction that was enough to drive Remington nuts. He could feel Pembroke's hands on his skin as he explored what he could of his body, and he was doing the same, touching Pembroke's smooth back and feeling the scars there, kneading his bubbly ass cheeks, and rubbing his fingertips against his hairy thighs.

On his way up, he tickled his fingers along Pembroke's crack. It was easy to find Pembroke's hole, and he loved the way Pembroke's breath hitched as he gently circled it with one finger.

Pembroke thrust harder against Remington, making him see stars. He slid down closer, settling between Remington's open legs. Remington wrapped his thighs around Pembroke's body, hooking his ankles together so Pembroke couldn't go far.

He doubted Pembroke wanted to, anyway.

This was heaven. It was everything Remington had ever dreamed of, and as Pembroke shuddered on top of him and rubbed against his body, he knew he'd do everything in his power to give this man anything he could ever wish for. Pembroke deserved to be spoiled and loved, and he'd chosen Remington to do so. It was incredibly humbling, and Remington wouldn't disappoint him.

"I'm coming," Pembroke murmured in a broken voice.

He shuddered, and Remington clung to him, holding him through his orgasm. The way his cock jerked against Remington's drove Remington wild, and as soon as Pembroke was done, he pushed a hand between them and wrapped his fingers around his cock. He jacked himself off furiously, needing Pembroke to smell like him.

Like *them*.

When he came, Pembroke did what Remington had done earlier. He held him close and kissed him, murmuring sweet words in his ear. He'd never get bored of telling Pembroke that he loved him. He wasn't planning on stopping anytime soon.

Eventually they had to separate, but they didn't go far. Pembroke rolled to the other side of the bed, looking pleasure drunk. He watched Remington as he got out of bed and went to the bathroom, where he quickly cleaned up. He grabbed a towel, dampened it in the sink, then headed back to the bedroom, where Pembroke was already half asleep. While Remington cleaned them up, Pembroke murmured a few things, but Remington didn't pay attention. He doubted Pembroke was saying anything that made sense.

Pembroke was exhausted. He was still recuperating from what had happened to him over the past three years and was dealing with nightmares and probably PTSD. He'd need a lot of support and time to heal, and Remington was ready to support him through all of it.

His phone vibrated in his jeans before he got into bed, so he snatched it up and settled next to Pembroke. His boyfriend wrapped himself around him like an octopus as soon as his ass touched the mattress, and Remington smiled. It was like Pembroke feared he'd disappear if he wasn't clinging to him.

He wrapped an arm around Pembroke's shoulders and held him close as he unlocked his phone and saw that Ryland had texted him.

*You're my best friend, and I trust you to take care of the most important person in my life. I knew Pembroke would eventually fall in love with someone, and I'm glad it's you.*

Remington was glad it was him, too.

# CHAPTER SEVEN

There was a bounce in Pembroke's step, even though the meeting he was about to attend didn't call for it.

The last thing he wanted was to talk about Fulton and Pamela, but he agreed that it was time to do something about them and the auction house. He wanted that part of his life to be over permanently, to be able to stop looking over his shoulder every time he was out of pack territory, and to enjoy his life with Remington.

He grinned as he walked toward Cam's office. He still lived here with him and Toby, but it wouldn't be for long. He wanted to be with Remington as much as possible, and he'd been spending his nights there.

Ryland didn't seem to care. He'd told Pembroke that he just wanted him to be happy and behaved accordingly since Pembroke and Remington had talked to him.

It was incredible to see, and Pembroke had a hard time believing that had actually happened. His brother hadn't told him to choose between him and Remington. He'd told him to be happy, and if that meant Pembroke was with Remington, he was all for it.

Pembroke was, too.

The office door was open, so he walked in without knocking. Most of the people who would be at the meeting were already there, including Remington and Ryland. They were sitting in a corner, and Pembroke's heart jumped when he saw they'd saved him a chair. He made a beeline for it, flopping into it and leaning sideways to kiss Remington's cheek.

"Did I miss anything?" he asked.

"We haven't started yet."

He looked around the room. Cam was there with his hacker, Angus, and Everly, one of the rare shifters who lived there. From what Pembroke had heard, Everly was great with computers, too, and he'd been helping Angus uncover as much information on Pamela and Fulton as they could. One of Cam's betas was present, too. The older man looked like he wanted to be anywhere but here, but his loyalty was to his alpha, so here he was. Tyler and Matt were sitting close to Pembroke, softly talking as they waited. Cam's brother Bryson was sitting next to Mercer, along with the twin phoenix shifters and a few others. Pembroke didn't remember everyone's name yet, and trying to would give him a headache, so instead, he focused on Cam.

Everyone heard the front door open and close, and Pembroke sat up straighter in his chair. He blinked when he saw the man who came in and leaned closer to Remington. "Isn't that Matt's lawyer?"

Remington nodded. "He's in family law, but since he's involved in this, we thought it would be a good idea to have him here."

"Thank you, everyone, for being here today," the alpha said. "I suggest we get straight to the point." He looked at Remington. "Since you were the one who brought up this idea, why don't you introduce it?"

Remington sat up straighter in his chair. "I'm sure this is something we've all thought, but I believe that Pamela is so interested in Cora and Matt because she thinks they'll give her access to the pack so she and Fulton can kidnap the rare shifters who live here."

One of the twins snorted. "She can try, but she won't like what happens if she does."

Pembroke was pretty sure that was Carey. From what he

knew, Lennox was quiet, and his twin was not quiet at all.

"You can defend yourself and your partners, but not everyone here has the same ability. We want everyone to be safe, which means getting rid of them as soon as we can. Besides, even if we can keep the pack safe, what about the other shifters they've been kidnapping?"

"So what do we do?" Ryland asked. "I'm pretty sure I blew my cover when I bought Tyler. She knows he's here and that he's free, so she has to know I didn't buy him for the same reasons the others usually buy shifters."

"We could send someone else in," Cam suggested. "At the very least, we need the names of the regulars at the auctions. Angus and Everly have been looking into it, but even though Fulton is a slimy asshole, he's good at what he does. They're having a hard time finding out anything more than details."

"I can fund this, but I don't think I can go in again," Ryland said.

"I'll go," Preston said. Everyone turned to him. He didn't seem to care as he continued, "I've never met Pamela. I've never even met her lawyer, since we communicated through emails and phone calls. They both know my name, but that's the name I use at work."

"Do you have another one?" Pembroke asked.

Preston nodded. "I do. My family is quite wealthy. I didn't want any of that to influence my work, so I always used my mother's maiden name there. If I were to use my father's, Pamela would welcome me with open arms."

"It would be dangerous," Cam warned. "Especially since you're a rare shifter."

"But no one knows I am. My father is human, and my mother being a shifter is a well-kept secret. It would be dangerous, but as long as you don't expect me to go in there on my own, I think I can do it."

Pembroke wanted to ask what kind of shifter Preston was,

but it would be rude, so he kept his mouth shut.

"We can keep you safe," Remington promised. "Braden is eager to help again. Between our company and the pack, we have more than enough people to protect Preston and make sure nothing happens to him. We'll also have enough people to rescue any shifters Pamela and Fulton have caged when we decide to do so."

Pembroke shivered. He wasn't planning to go with them. Maybe he should, because he wanted to help the others there, but he didn't think he could face that place. It had been his personal hell for too long, and he'd be happy if he never saw it again. He was pretty sure Tyler felt the same. He'd been incredibly brave when he'd come with the others to rescue Pembroke, and no one would ask him to be a part of this, just like they wouldn't ask Pembroke. The two of them were out of this mess, and while Pembroke wanted to know what was happening, he wouldn't be participating.

Maybe that made him a coward, but he didn't care. Pamela and Fulton had hurt him too much, and now that he was finally leaving them behind, he didn't want to be forced to face them again. He felt it would undo all the work he'd done on himself to start healing, and he couldn't let that happen.

He wanted to be happy, dammit, and that meant staying away from those two monsters.

"We could use more people," Cam agreed. "I want to reinforce pack security. I won't let Pamela in anymore because I'm done allowing her to terrorize Tyler and Matt, but I wouldn't put it past her to sneak in. Besides, she's not stupid. She must know that we're aware of why she keeps visiting. She's probably planning to strike soon, so I want her out of pack territory before she decides it's the right time. Unfortunately, pack territory is extensive, and my guards aren't enough."

"I'll talk to Braden, and we'll work something out," Remington promised. "We all want to keep the pack safe."

Even Pembroke was ready to help. He might not want to face Fulton and Pamela again, but he could help patrol the area and make sure no one tried sneaking in. He'd be able to defend the pack in his hydra form, and he wanted to. Strange currents had brought him here and placed him in his mate's path, and he'd always be grateful.

The pack had welcomed him when he'd been at his lowest. It had become the place where he wanted to live the rest of his life and where he and his mate were settling down. He'd do anything to protect it and its inhabitants.

And if that meant reducing Fulton and Pamela to bloody pancakes, he would.

# ABOUT THE AUTHOR

Catherine is the creator of several series, most of them paranormal, including the Whitedell Pride Series and the Gillham Pack Series. While she graduated in translation, she decided to go the writer's way because it was more fun to create her own stories and characters.

She's been living in Italy for more than twenty years, but she's a daughter of the North — Belgium to be precise — and she misses it so much that she's already planning to move back.

She loves pizza — probably too much — her son, her pets, and of course, books. She sneaks some reading time into her schedule every time she has five minutes free from writing, demands from her various pets and son, and lastly, housework.

Connect with her:

lievens.catherine@gmail.com
BookBub: https://www.bookbub.com/authors/catherine-lievens
Website: https://authorcatherinelievens.com/
Facebook: https://www.facebook.com/catherine.lievens.9
Facebook Group: https://www.facebook.com/groups/411788002341528/
Twitter: https://twitter.com/authorCLievens
Newsletter: http://eepurl.com/c-uvKn

www.ingramcontent.com/pod-product-compliance
Lightning Source LLC
Chambersburg PA
CBHW060635130626
46555CB00002B/814